A HEAD AND SOME TALES

"What an ugly face!" The man's voice sounded behind Eddy Stone's right ear.

It was that face that started it all. None of the mess that followed would have happened if it hadn't caught Eddy Stone's eye on that Saturday afternoon.

"Imagine having to look at someone so hideous every day," the man continued.

"Yes," said his wife, sadly. "Just imagine."

Eddy was staring at the face in question. He didn't think "ugly" was the right word for it. Unusual, yes. Striking, certainly. It was a life-sized sculpture of a head made of red clay. It had a short curved nose and a long curled moustache, sharp eyes and a pointed chin.

It wore an expression that might have been a sly smile or a calculating frown – as though it had just come up with a clever joke, or a plan to get rid of an annoying insect. Eddy had been enjoying a sunny day with no school by riding his bike round the little seaside town of Tidemark Bay, where he lived with his mum and dad. Spring had sprung, and down by the harbour the shops and cafes were sprucing themselves up for the start of the tourist season. He had been watching the owners dusting floors and washing windows and touching up paintwork, when he had noticed a stream of people heading for the Community Centre and had gone to see what they were all doing.

There was a sign outside.

4

Tidemark Manor was a grand old house that stood proud on a hill above the bay. For the last few years it had stood proud and empty, and many people from the town had peered through the bars of the great iron gates at the end of its long tree-lined drive, wondering what was inside its walls. So there was quite a crowd in the Community Centre taking this opportunity to find out.

The Manor's last owner, Lady Madeleine Montagu, had been a famous traveller in her youth – which was now the best part of a hundred years ago. Souvenirs of her journeys were stacked on tables all around. There were dragon-shaped vases from China and

tribal masks from Africa and delicate tea sets from Japan and rich silks from India and a large pink plastic prawn waving a flag with the words "A Present From The British Seaside" on it.

Lady Madeleine Montagu hadn't just been a famous traveller, she'd been a famously eccentric one. No challenge was too bold for her, no plan too wild. Not for nothing had her chums called her Mad Monty. Eddy spotted a stack of old books in tattered covers. These were the tales of some of her wackiest journeys – *Through Russia by Rollerskate, A Madagascan Monocycle, Pedalo on the Limpopo* and *A Pogo Stick in Peru.*

Eddy flicked open the last one. There was a brown and white photo: in front of a tangle of plants a young woman on a spring-loaded contraption, hair and skirt flying, was bouncing out of the side of the picture in a blur.

Eddy would have liked to buy the books. He would have liked to buy loads of other stuff, too. But the one thing he really craved, more than any other, was the red clay head.

It was as though it was talking to him.

"Come on. You know you want me."

It would look great sitting on the shelf in his bedroom, Eddy thought. He wondered if he would be able to afford it. All he had was this week's pocket money.

He saw a man in a smart blazer with a badge on his lapel standing nearby. He must be something to do with the sale.

"Excuse me," he asked the man. "Can you tell me the price of this head?"

"Not yet, I can't," said the man. "This is an auction sale. It will be sold to the person who puts in the highest bid. You see the number on the card in front of it?"

Eddy did – 49.

"That means it is lot
number 49. You'll have to
wait till we've sold the first 48 lots,
and then you can try to buy it. Though if I were you, I'd
have a look round for something that's not quite as ugly."

"I won't change my mind," said Eddy. "That's the one
for me."

"Good afternoon, ladies and gentlemen." A man in a
grey suit was standing behind a tall desk. His voice cut
through the chatter in the room. "Welcome to this sale
of the contents of Tidemark Manor. We'll begin with
Lot 1 – a fine example of an antique mahogany pogo
stick. Who will start the bidding? Do I have two
hundred?"

He did. Someone raised their hand and the auction
began. Lot by lot, paintings and pottery and
paraphernalia were snapped up by eager buyers. And
then, at last, the auctioneer cried out, "Lot 49. Any
offers?"

If only Eddy had known what Lot 49 really was.

Then he would have realized how much trouble it
was going to cause.

Then he would have decided he did not want to take it home with him after all.

Then he would not have raised his hand to bid.

But he didn't.

So he didn't.

So he didn't.

So he did.

A LOT OF
JUNK

Eddy plonked a large cardboard box down on the kitchen table. The head peered out of the top of it.

"What is that ugly old thing?" his mum asked. "And what is it doing on my table?"

"I don't know why everybody thinks he's ugly," said Eddy. "But I'm glad they do, because it means that no one else wanted to buy him. So I got him really cheap."

"You paid money for him?" His mother sounded as though she thought that was not a good idea.

"There was a sale of stuff from Tidemark Manor. He was Lot 49. I know why they call them lots, now. It's because there was lots of other stuff that came with him. This whole boxful. I think they must have just pulled it out of a cupboard and put it on sale. I asked if

I could just take the head and leave the rest, but they told me it was all mine now and I had to take it away. I had to balance the box on my handlebars and wheel my bike home."

"I want you to take it away, too," said his mum. "Upstairs and into your room. Then wash your hands and come straight back down. Dad will be home from work any minute and dinner's nearly ready. And be nice to him. Sit and chat. He's got a lot on his plate right now trying to sort out the astronaut problem."

Eddy's mum and dad ran a business selling fancy dress outfits for pets. They were getting lots of complaints about their new astronaut set for dogs. Customers had found that dog breath steamed up the helmets, so their pets couldn't see and kept bumping into things.

Over dinner, Eddy's dad had a lot to say about how he was trying to find a way to fix the problem, so it wasn't until much later that Eddy was able to sit on his bed and take a proper look through the cardboard box. He put the head up on his bookshelf and started to pull out the rest of Lot 49.

There was a faded cook's apron, with a pattern of pink roses. And a pair of large green wellington boots.

11

So far, so useless.
Then a layer of
newspaper that had
been used as packing.
It was yellow and brittle
and crumbled in his hand.

There was something else underneath, something that
had been rolled in a cloth and then tied securely with
string. Eddy wondered what was inside. Someone must
have thought it needed wrapping up to stop it getting
damaged. Maybe it was valuable? The knots were tight,
but he managed to work them loose.

He eagerly unrolled the cloth.

And was instantly disappointed.

It was a table lamp. A really hideous old-fashioned table lamp made of bright orange pottery, topped by a shade of purple silk with lime-green tassels. The colours shrieked at each other. It would have walked away with first prize in an ugly competition.

Eddy was just wondering what to do with it when it slipped from his grip, almost like it had jumped away from him. He clutched thin air as the lamp clattered to the floor with a crunch. The pottery base cracked and broke into pieces.

There was a faint fug and a strange smell in the air. It was ripe and rank and sweaty, and made him feel a bit dizzy.

He wrapped the pieces in the cloth and put them in his wastepaper basket.

Was that it then? Everything out of the cardboard box?

No. There was an old toothbrush, its bristles bent and brown. Ugh! Straight into the wastepaper basket with that, too.

Apart from the head, it looked like Lot 49 was just a lot of junk. But there was one more thing, right in the bottom of the box. Its outside was dark leather, carved with a scrolling pattern and dotted with metal studs. It was fastened with a metal clasp. It took him a moment to realize that it was a book.

Perhaps this was something special. Something that would make the effort of carrying the cardboard box all the way home worthwhile.

Eddy snapped the clasp open. There was a note on the inside of the cover, in neat, elegant handwriting.

"*A souvenir,*" it read, "*of my last and strangest journey. As if I could ever forget one moment of it. MM.*"

MM. Madeleine Montagu. Eddy wondered what weird and wonderful trip she had been on. It would take quite something to make it her strangest one.

He turned the page. A sheet of loose paper fluttered out. There was more of Madeleine Montagu's writing on it. Was this the story of her amazing adventure?

"*Skirts - 2,*" he read. "*Blouses - 3. Sun hat.*"

No, it wasn't. It was a laundry list.

"*Boots - 2 pairs. Stick (stout).*"

No, not laundry. It must be things to pack for her trip. But it still wasn't interesting.

He looked through the book. This was more like it.

It was full of beautiful coloured drawings. A palace
with high walls. A man dressed in red and gold
sitting on a throne. A cave full of treasure. Someone
wearing artificial wings jumping from a tall tree. And
– Eddy took a sharp breath in surprise – a tall figure
in a black cloak whose face was just like the red clay
head that he had brought home.

Who was he? And what was the book about? Eddy
couldn't work it out. The writing underneath the
pictures was like nothing he had seen before –
curves and curls and squiggles that he couldn't
make head or tail of.

It was so frustrating not to be able to follow the story.

"I wish I could read the words in this book," Eddy said, "instead of that boring list of clothes that fell out of it."

 The strange smell
hit his nose again.
And then his eyesight
went funny.

The whole room seemed to ripple as though he was looking at a reflection in a pond and someone had just thrown a stone into the middle of it.

Was it the stink that did it? Maybe he was just getting tired. It was late. He had better put the book down and go to sleep.

But he didn't do that.

Because when he looked at the book again, something very strange had happened. The curves and curls and squiggles on the pages in front of him suddenly made sense, just as if they were perfectly ordinary letters. He went back to the start and began to read.

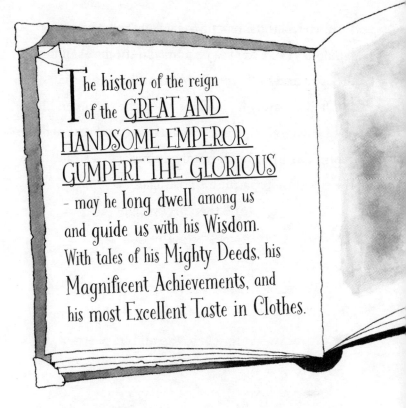

The history of the reign of the <u>GREAT AND HANDSOME EMPEROR GUMPERT THE GLORIOUS</u> - may he long dwell among us and guide us with his Wisdom. With tales of his Mighty Deeds, his Magnificent Achievements, and his most Excellent Taste in Clothes.

This, thought Eddy, sounds good. And he carried on with the story of the Emperor, and the beautiful palace that he had built, and the exotic treasures that he filled it with. And when Eddy came to the picture of the figure in the black cloak whose face looked just like the red clay head, he gasped again as he discovered that this was a mighty genie who performed great feats of magic at the Emperor's command.

It was all too fantastic to be true, but it was a fabulous tale. Eddy read and read until his eyelids drooped and sleep got the better of him.

He had barely nodded off when the statue on his shelf shivered. One eye popped open, and scanned the room. The lips turned briefly upwards in a smile, and the eye closed again.

YOU CAN'T ALWAYS GET WHAT YOU WANT

While Eddy was reading his book, it was Saturday evening in Tidemark Bay. Of course, it was Saturday evening in lots of other places as well, because that's how Saturday evening works. But in Tidemark Bay, Saturday evening got far more interesting than it did anywhere else.

Jeremy Grubb, for example, was getting ready to go out to the Tidemark Bay Over-50s Shepherd's Pie and Disco Evening. His bald head shone in the bathroom mirror as he checked that his shirt collar was neatly tucked into his jumper. He sighed. How he wished that he had all his hair again.

He clutched hold of the basin, feeling a little dizzy as his eyesight wobbled. When his eyes cleared again, he could see some sort of pale fuzz, like babies have, all over the top of his head. He blinked and looked again. Not only was the fuzz there, but it was getting longer. And thicker. And darker.

Within seconds there was hair hanging down over his ears. And then his neck. And then tumbling over his shoulders. Soon it reached all the way to the floor. And still it carried on, until Jeremy Grubb was standing in a pool of his own hair that reached halfway up to his knees and spread out across the bathroom floor.

Then, at last, it stopped.

Jeremy Grubb scrabbled in the bathroom cabinet and pulled out a pair of nail scissors. He snipped at a strand of hair.

The locks parted and then, to his astonishment, joined together again where he had cut them.

All his hair was back. All his hairs, that is. Every centimetre of every single one that had grown on his head in his entire life. And they were back to stay.

Eight-year-old Sophie Pinkerton was already in her bed at Harbour View Cottage. Her mum had sent her upstairs with no pudding as punishment for feeding her sprouts to the new puppy underneath the dinner table. But Sophie was still wide awake. And still fuming. It was so unfair. How could she have guessed that the puppy would like sprouts so much that he jumped up on the table to eat them off everyone else's plates? Or that they would all come back up just as fast as he had gobbled them down?

It wasn't her fault. If anyone should be punished it was the puppy. Or whoever invented sprouts in the first place. They had no excuse.

It was strawberry ice cream for pudding. She loved strawberry ice cream. She wished she had some now.

In fact, she wished she had the biggest bowl of strawberry ice cream in the world.

A couple of streets away, Sharon Dibble was all dressed up and about to leave for a night out with some friends. She was staring into the cupboard where she kept her shoes. They all looked old and drab. Not right for tonight. She wished she had some really, really nice shoes.

A strange feeling washed over her. She shook her head to try and clear it. There was a pair of smart, shiny black high heels on her shoe rack. She was sure they hadn't been there a minute ago. But they were exactly the shoes she wanted. She slipped them on. They were a perfect fit.

She headed for the front door.

"Lovely carpet," said a small voice.

"And I like the colour of these walls," said another. "Very soothing."

Sharon stood stock-still.

"You've got very shapely feet," said the first voice.

"And nicely trimmed toenails," added the second.

Sharon thought she was probably losing her mind. It sounded like her shoes were talking.

She bent down towards them.

"Is that you?" she asked in a trembling voice.

"I'm sorry," said the first shoe. "Did we startle you?"

"We'd never want to do that," said the second.

Sharon decided that she wasn't going to go out that night. She would ring and tell her friends that she was feeling a bit odd.

She went into the front room, sat down and turned the TV on.

"This programme looks good," said the first shoe.

"Yes, super," said the second.

And they carried on like that all night. Both shoes, being nice about everything.

Really, **really** nice shoes.

At number 26 Culvert Avenue, Mrs Daphne Venables switched on her TV to watch the draw for the Mega Lottery. She wished, just like she did every week, that the numbers on her ticket would match the six balls that were about to pop out of the machine.

Two doors away at number 22, her neighbour Harry Hodges did exactly the same. And so did Colin Clutterbuck round the corner at 6 Homeward Lane, Nikki Cheung up the hill at 19 Hollybush Avenue, and forty-two other people at forty-two other addresses in Tidemark Bay.

Seven minutes later, Mrs Daphne Venables heaved a deep sigh. "Ah, well," she said to her husband, "no good. I'll have to go back to work at the bun factory for another week." She was about to throw her losing ticket into the bin, when something odd about it caught her eye.

"That's strange," she said. "These aren't my usual numbers on this ticket. Hang on – seven, nine, thirty-two, thirty-nine, forty-three and forty-eight. Oh my goodness! I'VE WON!!!! I'VE WON THE MEGA LOTTERY!!!! I've got to phone and tell them!"

Strangely enough, at that precise moment, the very same words were being shouted by her neighbour Harry Hodges at number 22, Colin Clutterbuck round the corner at 6 Homeward Lane, Nikki Cheung up the hill at 19 Hollybush Avenue, and forty-two other people at forty-two other addresses in Tidemark Bay.

One of the people in Tidemark Bay who had not won the Mega Lottery that night was Maurice Burbage. Maurice had not even bought a ticket. He wasn't interested in such vulgar contests. Maurice's passion was the theatre. For over forty years he had been a leading figure in the Tidemark Bay Amateur Dramatic Society. Tonight he had gone to bed early to learn the lines for his next starring role. He was determined to be word-perfect, and to silence the sniping doubters who had said that he was too old to play Romeo.

Not old, he had told them. Experienced. And though he might not *be* eighteen years old any more, he could still *play* eighteen years old. It was what they called acting, my dears. And he was a very, very good actor. He was quite sure of that.

He often wondered how far he might have risen if he had taken it up professionally. By now he could be a huge star, onstage in one of the great theatres – maybe the National Theatre itself. How marvellous that would be. Yes, he wished he was onstage at the National Theatre. And he drifted off to sleep.

And that was Saturday evening.

And Sunday morning got even stranger.

YOU DON'T ALWAYS WANT WHAT YOU GET

On Sunday morning, the sun rose as usual over the harbour in Tidemark Bay. Usually after it rose, it spent a few minutes having a bit of a glint on the surface of the water in the harbour, while a handful of boats bobbed up and down. But not today. Today there was no glinting. Or bobbing, come to that. The water was not its usual self. It had turned thick and icy and creamy overnight. Thick and icy and creamy and bright strawberry pink, inside the gigantic dish of the harbour wall. Sophie Pinkerton didn't know it yet, but she had got her wish. Sitting slap in the middle of the harbour, the crew of the yacht *Saucy Sue* did know it, and they were not happy. What they were instead, was stuck.

Maurice Burbage woke in a cold sweat. He had had a terrible dream in the night. A dream that was every actor's worst nightmare.

He was standing on a stage in a glare of spotlights, wearing only his pyjamas. Beyond the lights was darkness – a darkness that he knew was filled with a thousand pairs of eyes staring right at him. All the other actors were looking at him, waiting. But he had no idea what he was supposed to say or do. He didn't even know which play he was in. It was horrible. The memory of it made him feel sick. Thank goodness it was only a dream.

He turned on the radio by his bed. It was the news.

"...at the National Theatre are trying to find out how a member of the public managed to walk onstage during a performance last night," said the newsreader. "The man, who appeared to be wearing a pair of pyjamas, stood still for a few seconds, then shouted, 'Help! Mummy!' before running into the wings. He disappeared before anyone could catch him. And fi—"

Maurice Burbage turned the radio off again. Then he pulled his duvet over his head, stuck his thumb in his mouth and quietly sobbed.

"How embarrassing!" said Mrs Daphne Venables,
who was also listening to the news. She was sitting down
to breakfast with her husband Geoffrey, still brimming
with excitement from last night's Mega Lottery win.

"—nally," the newsreader newsread, "the Mega
Lottery has cancelled payments on last night's draw after
it received claims for 46 winning tickets, all from the
small seaside town of Tidemark Bay."

"What?" said Mrs Venables.

"They can't do that," said Mr Venables.

"We have a telephone interview now with the Mega
Lottery's mathematics advisor, Professor Felix Fermat,"
the newsreader continued.

"It is impossible to have 46 winners from a single
town unless either the ticket machine is faulty or it is
the result of a criminal plot. In either case the result is
up the spout," the Professor told the programme's one
million listeners.

"But I won," said Mrs Venables.

"Course you did," said Mr Venables.

"You say impossible," said the newsreader, "but isn't
there a small chance that it could happen naturally?"

"Only a teeny weeny tiny winy itsy bitsy fraction of a shred of a sliver of a chance," said the Professor. "One in a million billion trillion umptillion. It is about as likely that the sausage I am about to eat for breakfast will stand up on the plate and sing the *Hallelujah Chorus*."

"It's so unfair," said Mrs Venables.

"What do experts know anyway?" said Mr Venables. "I wish his sausage would do exactly that and teach him a lesson."

A million radio listeners suddenly heard a shrill scream, a clatter of cutlery dropping to the floor, and footsteps disappearing rapidly into the distance.

"Professor?" said the newsreader.

"Are you still there?"

But all was silent.

Apart from a tiny,

high voice.

"HALLELUJAH!" it chirped.

"HALLELUJAH!

HALLELUJAH!

HALL-AY-AY-LOO-JAH!"

✳ ✳ ✳

Eddy Stone was still asleep when all this happened. When he eventually woke, he found his new book on the bed next to him. The loose sheet of paper with Madeleine Montagu's packing list had slipped out of it. He picked it up to put it back inside. But something wasn't right. The words on the paper wouldn't settle properly in front of his eyes. He remembered that the list had started with "skirts", "blouses" and "sun hat". But now it looked like "squats", "bruises" and "gunboat".

Weird.

He looked around. There was another book nearby – one from his school library about the Norman Conquest. Except that now, when he tried to read the title on the cover, it looked like Normal Cow Test. He opened it. The words danced in patterns of nonsense.

Weirder.

He tried the leather-bound book, and found he could still read the stories about Emperor Gumpert and his genie perfectly. So that squiggly writing was no problem. He remembered that he had made a wish that he could read this new book instead of the packing list. It was as if that had worked out – just not quite as he had expected. Especially the "instead" part. It wasn't just the packing list that he couldn't read – it was everything that used the normal alphabet. Nothing written in his own language made sense any more.

But wishes didn't come true, did they? Not in real life. Not like that.

He went downstairs, poured himself a bowl of cereal for breakfast, and plonked himself down to watch TV in the front room.

His dad was already up and about. He was wearing one of his day-off shirts – turquoise with big bright red polka dots all over it. Eddy had never liked it.

But his dad wasn't behaving like it was a day off. He was bustling round in a hurry. He came into the front room, a slice of jammy toast gripped between his teeth.

"I'm off then," he said, through his breakfast.

"Where?" said Eddy.

"Work. I've had an idea. If I drill some holes in the astronaut helmets, that might stop them steaming up."

"But it's Sunday," said Eddy. "Rest day."

"I'm not doing it because I want to," said his dad.

"I'm doing it because I have to. It's alright for you. I wish I could sit around in front of the TV doing nothing all day."

A ripple ran through the room.

And then his dad turned into a sofa.

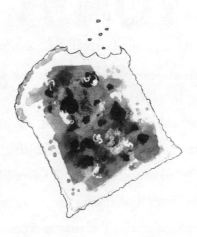

TOAST

Eddy had no idea what was happening.

The great detective Sherlock Holmes once said that when you have eliminated the impossible, whatever remains, however improbable, must be the truth. But to be fair to Eddy, Sherlock never saw anyone turn into a piece of furniture. And you would have to work your way through an awfully long list of possible explanations before you arrived at that one.

Eddy knew something strange had happened. One minute he was looking at his dad. The next minute he was looking at a sofa that he had never seen before. A sofa covered in a turquoise fabric with big red polka dots all over it. Just like his dad's shirt.

At first he thought his dad might be behind it.

"Dad?"

Then maybe that he had left the room.

"Dad?"

Then Eddy noticed something sticking out from between the seat cushions. It was a slice of jammy toast – a slice with a single bite taken out. It was only when he put that together with the turquoise and red pattern that the thoroughly improbable truth dawned on him.

"Mum!" he called. "Come quickly. I think Dad has turned into a sofa."

He heard her footsteps on the stairs.

"What was that?"

"I said…" He hesitated. It was ridiculous. But he had to say it again. "I think Dad has turned into a sofa."

His mother came into the room.

"I don't know where you got that thing from," she said, "but it will have to go. There's no space for it in here.

And those colours clash horribly with the curtains."

"I didn't put it there," said Eddy. "And it can't go. I think it's Dad."

"Very funny," his mother snapped. "We aren't all young people with time to be silly, you know. Some of us are grown-ups with too much to do." She sighed. "Sorry. I don't mean to be cross. I'd like to have time to be silly sometimes. You don't know how lucky you are. I wish I was young again like you."

The strange ripple passed through the room again, blurring everything in front of Eddy's eyes. When the view cleared, a teenage girl was standing in his mother's clothes. There was no mistaking who she was. She looked just like she did in the wedding photo on the dressing table in his parents' bedroom. Or maybe a bit younger.

"I feel dizzy," she said. She sat down on the turquoise sofa.

"Mum?" said Eddy. "Are you okay?"

"I don't know," she answered. "My head feels very strange. And why are you calling me mum?"

"Because that's who you are," said Eddy.

"Don't be daft," she said. "You're almost as old as me. How could I possibly be your mother?"

"But—" Eddy began. He didn't know what to say next. His mother didn't just look young again, he realized. She really was young again. And he reckoned that meant she had no memory of anything that had happened since she was a teenager.

"What's the last thing you can remember?" Eddy asked.

"I was working in my mum and dad's greengrocer's shop," she said. "Like every Saturday. And I've got a date tonight with the boy from the fish shop next door. He's nice."

Eddy had heard this story before – how his mum and dad first got together. He thought about telling his mother the truth – that she had married the nice boy from the fish shop and years later here they all were. But he realized that when he got to the bit where he had to explain that the nice boy from the fish shop had just turned into a sofa, and she was now sitting on him, it really wasn't going to help things. His mother was confused enough as it was.

"Where are we?" she said. "I don't recognize it."

She was starting to sound upset. He had to think of something fast.

"You are in a place called Tidemark Bay," he said. "You had a little accident and you've lost your memory." That was all true, at least. "You need to sit here quietly and rest until it gets better."

That calmed her down.

"My memory," she said. "Yes. It is all a bit fuzzy. Like there are big holes in it. I think I might have a nap."

"Good idea," said Eddy. "The other sofa would be better though. More comfortable for you."

Probably more comfortable for the sofa she was sitting on as well, he thought. He wondered if his dad felt squashed.

What was going on?

And how on earth could he put it right and get his mum and dad back?

WISHES

It was all to do with wishes.

And then there was the statue. And the picture in the book of a genie that looked just like it.

They had to be connected.

How or what or why, Eddy had no idea. But what else could it be?

He raced upstairs to his bedroom.

The statue looked down at him from his bookshelf.

"Our wishes only started coming true when I brought you home," Eddy said. "Well, now I wish everything was back just how it was before."

He waited. There was no ripple. No anything. He looked at the front of his book about the Norman Conquest. This time the title looked like Formal Omelettes. He still couldn't read it properly. Nothing had changed.

"Just stop it!" he yelled at the statue, his voice cracking with desperation. He had to get his parents back. "Stop it now!"

"I can't."

It was a weedy, reedy voice. And it didn't come from the statue. It came from inside Eddy's wardrobe.

Eddy threw open the wardrobe doors.

Something green and flimsy flitted back through the gap between a couple of hanging shirts.

"Shhhh!" it said. "I'm hiding."

"Oh!" said Eddy. "Sorry."

He shut the wardrobe doors again.

Wait a minute.

"What do you mean you're hiding?" He yanked the doors open for a second time.

"It's odd." The green thing peeped cautiously out from behind a pair of Eddy's trousers. "I spent all that time longing to get free from the lamp, but now that it's broken and I'm out, I feel completely undressed. You haven't got a vase or a jar that I could slip into, have you?"

"You were in the lamp?" said Eddy.

"For over a hundred years," said the green thing.

"Hang on," said Eddy. "Are you a genie?"

"Don't talk to me about genies," said the green thing. "It was a genie who trapped me. And anyway, do I look like a genie?"

"I can't tell," said Eddy. "Not while you are behind those trousers. Why don't you come out where I can see you?"

"Well…I suppose." The green thing slipped cautiously out from its hiding place. Eddy found himself looking at an elderly man with a bushy beard and eyebrows. He was dressed in a long gown decorated with stars and crescent moons, and wore a tall pointed hat on his head. As well as being bright green from top to bottom, he was flat and completely see-through, as if he was made of tissue paper.

"So," said the figure. "What do I look like now?"

"A wizard?" said Eddy.

"Quite right. Wizard Witterwort, that's me. At least, it was, until the Genie took away my body and stuck me in a lamp. That genie." He wafted a transparent arm in the direction of the clay head on Eddy's bookshelf. "I wish more than anything that I could get my body back."

"Why did he do that?" said Eddy.

"I annoyed his master, Emperor Gumpert."

"He was in my book," said Eddy, "Gumpert the Glorious."

"Gumpert the Glutton, more like," said Wizard Witterwort. "He was always stuffing his face. He was so fat you could have rolled him down a hill like a giant ball. That's what got me into trouble. I was young and looking to make my way in the world. I thought I'd be able to get into his good books by casting a surprise spell that made him lose weight."

"What happened?" said Eddy. "Didn't it work?"

"On, no, it worked. He lost lots of weight. I cast my spell, and both his legs fell off. Gumpert was furious. He ordered his genie to stick his legs back on, and then punish me by removing every last bit of my body, stuffing me in that lamp and slapping a curse on me. Then Gumpert shoved the lamp in a cupboard at the palace and left me there for years until someone called Mad Monty turned up."

"Mad Monty," said Eddy. "You mean Madeleine Montagu?"

"That's her," said the Wizard. "She wanted some souvenirs. She thought a wizard in a lamp was very exotic. The Emperor couldn't wait to get rid of me. He said some very rude things about me. I could hear every word."

"You said something about a curse?" said Eddy.

"Yes," said Wizard Witterwort. "A curse on anyone who let me out."

"You mean me," said Eddy. "I broke the lamp."

"The curse is that now I am out of the lamp, I have to grant one wish to everyone in your town," said Wizard Witterwort. "Hang on – I've got one coming in. The lady across the street from you has just wished that her house was a lot bigger. Let's see…"

Eddy knew his neighbour. She had a small cottage and a large family. He wasn't surprised that she had wished they had more space.

"Here goes," said Wizard Witterwort. His wispy green fingers fluttered in the air, and a ripple flowed out of him and across the street.

As Eddy watched from his bedroom window, the house opposite began to grow. Every brick in its walls, every tile on its roof, every door, and every pane of glass began to get larger, as if the house was a picture painted on a balloon that was being inflated. And like a balloon, when the house reached its neighbours on the left and the right, it stopped spreading sideways but carried on bulging upwards and outwards. It grew until every part of it was three times as big as when it had started, and its front wall had spread right across the street. The huge knocker on its massive front door was almost touching Eddy's bedroom window.

"There," said Wizard Witterwort. "One bigger house. All sorted."

"Sorted?" said Eddy. "They won't even be able to open the front door. They'll need to fetch ladders to get up the stairs. When she said she wanted a bigger house she meant more rooms. Normal-sized rooms. Not this."

He was interrupted by the honking of a car horn, and an angry voice shouting, "Oi! You can't park that house there. Get it shifted."

"That's not what she wished," said the Wizard. "Bigger means bigger. Oh, it's always like this. I try to do

43

what people want but it turns out wrong."

"I can see why getting a wish from you is a curse now," said Eddy. "It's just like my mum and dad and me. We all got what we asked for. But not what we wanted. Can you just put it all right?"

"No," said the Wizard. "Those are the rules of the Genie's curse. I can't do any magic except to perform one wish per person. And no one can wish something back again once it's done."

"But things can't stay like this," said Eddy. "It's a disaster. My dad's a sofa, my mum's lost half her life, and goodness knows what else has happened all round the town."

"Nothing I can do, I'm afraid," said Wizard Witterwort. "But I have got a message. Mad Monty used to tell me the same thing every night. She said that if anyone ever let me out, they must find the secret room at Tidemark Manor. That was their only chance to get things back to normal."

"Why?" said Eddy. "What's in there?"

"That," said the Wizard, "is something she never told me."

BE CAREFUL WHAT YOU WISH FOR

Eddy didn't leave the house straight away.

He found an empty vase to keep Wizard Witterwort snug.

He checked that his mum was sleeping comfortably.

He turned the TV on quietly for his dad to watch. His dad always liked a snack while he was in front of the telly, so Eddy slipped a couple of digestive biscuits down the back of his seat cushions.

And then he squeezed his bike out through the narrow gap between the front door and the giant house opposite, and set off for Tidemark Manor.

As he cycled up the street, all around him people who knew nothing of the Wizard and the curse were finding that their wishes were suddenly coming true. And that you really should be careful what you wish for.

Gary Sprott was sitting in bed playing an army game

on his console. He wished he had a real tank. He
imagined the look on his classmates' faces as he drove
it into school. Right into school. CRUNCH! How brilliant
would that be? He was astonished to find that he
suddenly did have a tank, and that he was sitting in it in
his bedroom. He wasn't in his bedroom for long, though.

The three-hundred-year-old floorboards of his family's
cottage had never been designed to hold up anything as
heavy as this great lump of metal, and they certainly
weren't going to start now. With a CREAK and a CRASH,
Gary Sprott suddenly found himself sitting in his tank
in the living room. And, seconds later, in the cellar.

Sophie Milldew was in the middle of getting her kids' breakfast ready and stopping the dog from eating her toast and loading the washing machine and hunting for her house keys when the phone rang. She wished she had an extra pair of arms. Showing remarkable self-control in the circumstances, she only screamed for the next three hours. And then went upstairs to cut extra armholes in some of her tops.

Dylan Plimpsoll was scanning the internet for tips on how to get a girlfriend. He was keen on a pretty assistant who worked at the corner shop, but she never seemed to notice him. A website said that girls often liked boys who made them laugh. That was something that Dylan wasn't very good at. His jokes always fell flat. He wished that people laughed at the things he said.

He went to the corner shop to buy some milk. He said, "Good morning," to the pretty girl. She giggled. He commented on the weather. She chuckled. Feeling more confident than ever before, he asked what her name was. She chortled as she told him. It was going so well, Dylan thought. Just like the website said. He gathered his courage and asked her out for a date. And then the pretty girl threw back her head and laughed out loud. She laughed and laughed and laughed, and was still laughing when Dylan Plimpsoll turned tail and ran, red-faced, out of the shop.

Round the corner, little six-year-old Gregor Samsa was thrilled when he woke up and found he had changed in his bed into a giant beetle.

Eddy cycled up to the iron gates at the end of the long gravel drive that led up to Tidemark Manor. He got off his bike to push the gates open.

"Oi! Mate!" A voice interrupted his thoughts.

He looked around. There was no sign of anyone.

"Mate!" There it was again.

"Oi! Cloth ears!"

"Down here, mate!"

He looked down. A small group of rabbits were gathered round a bush just to his right.

"Got any carrots?"

"Or lettuce, mate?"

Talking rabbits. Who on earth had wished for them?

"Sorry, no," he said, shoving the gates open.

"What about parsley?"

"Yeah, we like parsley, mate."

"I haven't got anything," said Eddy. "But I passed a big patch of dandelions just back there."

"Dandelions? Thanks, mate."

"You're a mate, mate."

The rabbits hopped away. Eddy wheeled his bike through the gate, and closed it behind him. Then he set off up the drive towards Tidemark Manor.

No one in town knew who had bought the house. He wondered who the new owners would turn out to be – and what they would say when he asked to poke around and hunt for the secret room.

HEN

Tidemark Manor had a long history. Its oldest
parts had been standing for hundreds of years
– though some of them were now leaning
alarmingly and looked like they might
decide to have a good lie-down at any
moment. It wasn't quite a stately
home – it was too jumbled and
crumbling for that. But it was certainly
grand. The entrance porch where Eddy was
now standing, its eight thick classical
columns each two storeys tall, was as big as
most people's houses.

Someone had hung a label marked
"Pull!" on a piece of string that dangled
down by the massive front door.

Eddy pulled.

He heard a whirring noise above his head. He looked up and saw that an electric fan sitting on a windowsill had started to blow air into the fat end of a metal funnel. The funnel's thin end was connected by a stretch of hosepipe to a curved brass horn that suddenly let out a loud **HONK!** like a startled goose.

The window opened, and a voice yelled "Hang on!" as a hand reached out and turned the fan off. The HONK faded to silence.

"Coming!" the voice added, as the window rattled shut again.

After a few seconds Eddy heard footsteps from inside the house.

The front door opened.

It was a girl. A girl about his age, wearing a blue boiler suit and a smear of thick, dark oil across one cheek.

"Excuse the mess. We haven't moved in properly yet. Can I help you?"

"I hope so. My name's Eddy – Eddy Stone – and…"

"Hen," said the girl.

"Where?" said Eddy turning to look behind him.

"No," said the girl. "That's my name. Hen. At least, that's what I like people to call me. My proper name is Henrietta, but I don't use that."

"I think it's a nice name," said Eddy. "Maybe a bit old-fashioned. Is that why you don't use it?"

"No," said Hen. "I don't use it because my surname is Crumb. My parents thought they had a sense of humour. Unfortunately for me. Every time I introduce myself as Henrietta Crumb someone says something stupid like 'Who ate the rest of the loaf?' as if it's a big joke. If I had a coin for every time someone had laughed at my name, I'd be almost as rich as my dad."

"And I suppose he must be very rich if he has bought this place."

"Rolling in it," said Hen. "Have you heard of Crumb's Crunchy Snacks?"

"Who hasn't?" said Eddy. "The most fun you can have with a potato, as it says on the packets."

"Well that's us," said Hen.

"Really?" said Eddy. "I'm a big fan of your Cheeze'n'Beanzy Bakes."

"I think they're stupid. When I grow up I'm going to be an engineer and make something useful."

"Did you make this?" said Eddy, pointing at the "Pull!" sign.

"Yes," said Hen. "When we started to move in a

couple of days ago I found that the old doorbell wasn't working. Like a lot of things in this place. So I rigged up that device from a few bits that came in our first load of packing cases."

"It's very clever," said Eddy.

"Not really," said Hen. "I need to work out a modification so it switches itself off again. Then it might be quite clever."

"Well, I think it's clever now," said Eddy.

"Thank you," said Hen. "If there's something you want to talk about, I'm afraid my mum and dad aren't here right now. They've gone away to meet the architect to discuss what they want to do with this place. It's just me and my brother at home."

"No problem," said Eddy. "I'm happy just to talk to you. In my experience, grown-ups don't always listen when you want to tell them something a bit out of the ordinary. And what I want to say is – well – pretty weird."

"Stop," said Hen. "I've got a full portion of weird going on here already. I don't think I could handle any more."

"What do you mean?" said Eddy.

"Come in," said Hen, "and I'll show you."

BONKERS

"Listen to me, Babes – I cannot go around dressed like this."

Eddy stared at the figure who was speaking. She was standing by a pile of packing cases in one of the many downstairs rooms at Tidemark Manor. She was about his height, and wearing a plain white coat that went down to her knees. Her face, all big lips and eyes and a tiny turned-up nose, was strangely smooth and had a distinctly orange tint. She reminded Eddy of a doll – but one that had grown five times taller and come to life.

"It's my mum's old doll," said Hen. "She has grown five times taller and come to life."

"I've got a name, Babes," said the doll.

"So have I," said Hen, "and it's not Babes."

"I'm Modern Model Mitzee," the doll said to Eddy. "Two ees."

"Pleased to meet you," said Eddy. "I'm Eddy."

"Is this your boyfriend?" Mitzee said to Hen. And then added quietly, "You could do a lot better, Babes. You just need to smarten yourself up."

"He's not my boyfriend," said Hen. "And I don't want to smarten myself up."

"I can see why you find this weird," said Eddy.

"And upsetting," said Hen. "Partly because it breaks every rule of science that I know, and partly –" she whispered into Eddy's ear – "because she's not very nice. And she's got really old-fashioned ideas."

"But I *do* want to smarten myself up!" The doll let out a yelp of complaint, and stamped her foot. "Thirty-six different outfits you can buy for me. I can be anything – tennis pro, show jumper, movie star. So why am I standing here in this horrible scratchy thing?"

"Because I wanted you to look like a scientist," said Hen, "and you can't buy an outfit for that, so I had to lend you my white coat."

"Scientist?" said Mitzee. "Not if it means dressing like this, Babes. I haven't even got proper shoes. Look."

Eddy looked. It was true. She was wearing blue plastic bags fastened round her ankles with elastic. "They use them in laboratories," said Hen. "So they don't bring in dirt." "Where's the glamour?" said Mitzee. "Where's the colour?" "Let me guess," Eddy said to Hen. "You made a wish and – POOF! – she came to life." "How did you know that?" said Hen. "Because people's wishes are coming true all over town," said Eddy. "But they aren't turning out like people expect." "Mine didn't," said Hen. "I was feeling lonely. Moving home and leaving all my friends.

Mum going away. I just wished I had someone to talk to. This isn't exactly what I wanted."

"It's not what I wanted either," said Mitzee. "No offence, Babes, but listening to you moaning on is really boring. Can't you talk about something interesting? Like me?"

"I'm trying to put this right," said Eddy.

"I can talk about myself for hours," said Mitzee.

"Put it right how?" said Hen.

"I'm really fascinating. I've got thirty-six outfits. And a pink beach buggy."

"I don't know yet," said Eddy. "But I think it starts here."

"And a pony!" said Mitzee. "Called Flash!" Then she stamped both feet and stomped out of the room.

"She's even worse than my brother," said Hen with a sigh. "But, where here? And while you are at it, why here? And I'd like a sensible, scientific explanation."

"Sorry," said Eddy. "The explanation isn't sensible or scientific. I bought some old stuff from this house in the sale yesterday. It turned out that it included a wizard called Witterwort with no body and a curse. He has to give everyone in town a wish. But his spells do unexpected things."

"You're right," said Hen. "About it not being sensible or scientific. But then neither is a walking, talking living doll. Go on."

"Who is this?" said a voice behind them.

Eddy turned. The boy standing in the doorway was a head taller than him.

"Eddy, meet my older brother," said Hen. "Crispy."

"Crispy?" said Eddy.

"It's Christopher," said the boy. "I hate it when she calls me that."

"Which is exactly why I do it, brother dear." Hen smiled. "First name Christopher, second name Philip. Get it? Chris P. Crumb. I told you my parents thought they had a sense of humour."

"Ouch," said Eddy.

"You were explaining?" said Hen.

"The Wizard gave me a message from the lady who used to live here," said Eddy. "There's a secret room. I don't know what's in it, but I think it's the way to put things right. Will you help me find it?"

"Normally," said Hen, "if anyone told me a story about wizards and spells, I would think they were bonkers. But what happened to Mitzee is bonkers too.

So, maybe what you have told me could just be true. So yes, I'll help you."

"Great," said Eddy.

"It could be difficult," said Chris P. "You see, the thing about secret rooms is that they are hidden and no one knows where they are."

"Thanks," said Hen. "Very helpful. I'll try to remember that."

"Any time," said Chris P.

"Have you seen anything odd around the place?" said Eddy. "Anything that might be a clue?"

"We haven't even looked round properly yet," said Hen. "There are so many rooms here. And miles of corridors."

"There's only one thing for it," said Eddy. "We'll have to explore it all. Tap on all the walls to find out if any are hollow, lift all the carpets to look for trapdoors, check all the cupboards for false backs, and…"

"That will take for ever," said Hen. "I've got a better idea. A scientific idea. Come on."

SENSIBLE
SCIENCE

"This", said Hen, "is how we can find the location of the secret room."

She spread a long roll of paper out on the floor. "It's a plan of the inside of the house. The estate agent gave it to us."

"It's no good looking for the secret room on there," said Chris P. "Because if it's on there it's not secret, so if it says there's a secret room it means there isn't one. And I have to stop thinking about that now. It's making my head hurt."

"Thank you", said Hen, "for sharing your brain with us. But I think you had better have it back now."

"No probs," said Chris P.

"The secret room won't be on this plan," said Hen, "because it's hidden away, and the estate agent won't have seen it when he was looking round and taking measurements on the inside. That's the point. If we check the outside of the house and find a bit sticking out somewhere that isn't on this drawing of the inside of the house, then that extra bit must be where the secret room is hidden."

"That sounds like it should work," said Eddy. "Let's go."

They started at the front of the Manor. Chris P took a bag from his pocket.

"I brought some snacks," he said. "Try one."

"Thanks," said Eddy. He pulled out a potato puff and popped it in his mouth. It tasted strangely sweet.

"It's a new flavour I've come up with. Ham and jam. What do you think? Does it need more jam?"

"Possibly," Eddy said. "Or better still – none."

"You don't like it?" said Chris P. "Well who asked you anyway?"

"You did," said Hen. "Ignore him, Eddy. He's always trying to come up with new flavours to impress Dad.

But never mind that now, we've got a job to do."

The front of the Manor was exactly as the plan showed. But things got more interesting round at the side. Over the centuries, different owners had added new rooms to the building, so this part was a hotchpotch of different-coloured stones and bricks.

Chris P peered at the plan.

"It says that room there is a scullery," he said. "Why would they have a room just for storing skulls? Hey – do you think they're still in there, all white and bony and grinning?"

"A scullery has nothing to do with skulls," Hen said with a sigh. "It's the room where they did the washing up."

"Ah," said Chris P. "I mean, yeah, I knew that really. I was just having a joke."

"This part of the house is the old kitchens," said Hen, reading the plan. "The bit in front of us was the butler's pantry."

"Well, I know what that was for," said Chris P. "Obviously. It's where the butler kept his—"

"Please don't say 'pants'," said Hen.

"Oh," said Chris P. "Alright, I won't. Anyway, all this is the part that Dad wants to knock down."

"What does he want to do that for?" said Eddy.

"So we can put in the new rooms," said Chris P. "The cinema. Swimming pool. Artificial beach. Tropical greenhouse. Indoor go-kart track. Pretty standard stuff, really."

"I wish Tidemark Bay had half of those things," said Eddy. "The town would be much more fun. Hang on a minute – look, up there. First floor. According to the plan of the inside there is a small bedroom with two windows. But that wall goes on a lot further on the outside."

"I see it," said Hen. "And you're right. Whatever is behind that bit of wall is not on the drawing. You might have found what we are looking for. Let's go and check it out."

They soon found the bedroom. And there it was – the wall on the inside that wasn't in the same place as the wall on the outside. It was flat and bare, except for a large, empty wooden bookcase.

"If the secret room really is behind there," said Hen, "there must be a way to get in."

"If this was a film," said Eddy, "that bookcase would revolve when you pulled on a handle that was disguised as a candlestick or something like that."

But there was no candlestick. Or anything else that could have been a handle in disguise. The room had been stripped down to plaster and boards.

"Maybe there's a bit of skirting board that you have to kick to open a hidden door," said Hen. "Or a loose floorboard that works as a lever when you stamp on it. It wouldn't be hard to build either of those."

KICKS and STAMPS echoed as they worked their way round the room. And found – nothing.

"We could just bash a hole in the wall," said Chris P. "We'll need something to hit it with."

"How about your head?" said Hen. "That should be big and thick enough."

"We can't just bash our way in," said Eddy. "We might damage whatever is on the other side."

"Or even bring the whole place crashing down," said Hen. "With a house as old as this there's no telling what would happen if we start hammering away."

"Perhaps we're looking in the wrong place," said Eddy. "What if you get in from somewhere else? The entrance can't be on the outside walls of the house. But maybe there's a way through from the corridor."

They went to check. There was a door in the wall where they thought the secret room was hidden. Hen opened it, and found a shallow cupboard, with shelves from floor to ceiling.

"I've already looked in there, Babes." Mitzee was walking along the corridor towards them. "It's empty. Like all the other cupboards. I can't find any decent clothes anywhere."

"We're not looking for clothes," said Hen. "She tugged the shelves and tapped around the inside of the cupboard. "This is all solid. No entrance here."

"Right," said Eddy. "We can't find a way into the secret room from this floor. So you must get in from up or down. What's above here?"

Hen checked on the plan.

"Just the roof," she said. "And it's almost flat here – no space for a way to crawl in."

"That only leaves below," said Eddy. "Let's check downstairs. There's got to be an entrance somewhere."

COUNTING

"This really is an **enormous** house, isn't it?" Eddy's voice echoed round the large room they had found down below. Eight tall windows ran across one long side, looking out over the gardens. There was a huge fireplace at each end, and hooks in the ceiling that must once have supported chandeliers.

"Ninety-four rooms," said Hen. "I counted them on the plan. Eighty-three fireplaces, four hundred and sixty-two windows, eighty-two chimneys, twelve baths…"

"Hang on," said Eddy. "How many fireplaces did you say?"

"Eighty-three."

"And how many chimneys?"

"Eighty-two."

"Which means…" said Eddy.

"… she can't count," said Chris P.

"…one of the fireplaces doesn't connect to a chimney," said Eddy. "So it can't work. Why would you have a fireplace that doesn't work?"

"Because you hired rubbish builders?" said Chris P.

"Or because it's not really a fireplace at all," said Eddy. "There are two in this room. The one at this end is right below where we were upstairs. And look, there's no sign of soot in it. It doesn't look like anyone has ever lit a fire here."

"So if this isn't a real fireplace," said Hen, "what is it?"

"An attractive decorative feature?" said Mitzee. "I can be an interior designer, you know. It's outfit number eleven. Yellow trouser suit and a sketchpad."

"Maybe that's all it is," said Eddy. "But maybe not." He climbed into the fireplace and peered upwards. "I could do with a torch."

"I always keep one in my toolbag," said Hen. She pulled one out of a canvas bag that was slung from her belt, and shone the light above Eddy's head. The beam picked out a dull glint of metal.

"That looks like the rung of a ladder," said Eddy.

"And look, there's another one above it. I think we've found our way in. If I can just…"

He jumped up to grab the bottom rung, arms outstretched. But his fingers didn't quite reach.

"I need something to stand on," he said.

"There's nothing around," said Chris P. "The furniture hasn't arrived yet."

"Come here and get on all fours," said Hen.

"Can't we just go and find a packing crate?" said Chris P.

"That would take time," said Hen. "And," she whispered to Eddy, "it wouldn't be half as much fun."

Chris P grumbled, but did what Hen had asked.

Eddy stepped up on his back.

"I can easily reach the bottom rung now," he said. "Here I go. I'd better take that torch."

"Be careful," said Hen. "There could be anything up there."

"Don't worry," said Eddy. "I will be." But she was right. He had been so excited at finding the ladder that he hadn't really thought about what it might lead to. He hoped there weren't going to be any nasty surprises up there.

He hauled himself up rung by rung. There were eight of them, and then the fake chimney stopped climbing and turned into a flat passageway. He crawled in cautiously and burrowed into the house, between the upstairs floor and the downstairs ceiling. The way was cramped and dusty and thick with spider webs.

After a short distance, his torchlight picked out a heavy iron bolt fixed to the wooden boards above his head. He looked more closely, and saw the outline of a trapdoor.

Eddy tugged at the bolt, waggling it from side to side to loosen the stiffness of years. It suddenly gave way. There was a creak of complaint from the hinges as he pushed the trapdoor until it opened wide enough for him to stick his head up and peep through. He shone the torch ahead of him and— YIKES!

The beam picked out a hideous face, bright red, wild-eyed and snarling.

The trapdoor clattered as Eddy let go and sat back, almost dropping the torch in surprise.

"Are you okay?" Hen's voice came faintly up from the fireplace.

"I'm not sure," Eddy yelled back. "Hang on."

He carefully opened the
trapdoor a crack, and shone
the torch through again.
The hideous face
glared back at him.

Along with several
others. Masks. *Phew!* They
were only masks, hanging on
the wall. He scanned around
with the torch.

There were pictures and pots and carvings and glinting metal objects hung and shelved and stacked wherever he looked.

"There's a room up here," he shouted. "It looks like no one has been in it for years. And it's full of stuff."

"What sort of stuff?" Hen asked.

"All sorts," said Eddy.

"Right," said Hen, "bend down again, Crispy. I'm going up."

"Ow," Chris P answered, as she planted her boots in the small of his back, and began to climb.

And "Ow" again, as Mitzee followed Hen.

"If there's loads of stuff there might even be some decent clothes," Mitzee said.

"Oof!" said Chris P, stretching his back out as he stood up. He grabbed for the bottom rung of the ladder.

"Hey, guys! I can't reach. Can somebody pull me up?"

But nobody was listening.

"Oh, well," Chris P said to himself. "Who wants to climb a stupid chimney anyway? And it's probably just a load of old rubbish up there."

BEDTIME

"It's just a load of old rubbish up here," said Mitzee.

"It doesn't look like rubbish to me," said Eddy shining the torch around the room. "These must all be things that Madeleine Montagu brought back from her travels."

"Pity she wasn't more interested in clothes," said Mitzee. "I can't see anything to wear. What are you looking for anyway?"

"I don't know," said Eddy. "The message just said we had to find a secret room. It didn't say why. Let's hope there's something in here that will tell us."

"There's a desk over there," said Hen. "Let's try that."

They found an open notebook on the desk. Eddy pulled down the sleeve of his jumper and wiped at the thick layer of dust that lay on it. There was writing underneath. Neat, elegant writing. Eddy bent forward to read it in the torchlight.

"It says 'Go wham in day concert'…"

"That's no help," said Hen. "It's just nonsense."

"No. It's me," said Eddy. "I'd forgotten. Since my wish the words get all muddled when I try to read normal letters. You have a look."

He handed the torch to Hen.

"*To whom it may concern,*" she read.

Only Wizard Witterwort and I know this room exists. If he has given you the message telling you to find it, it must mean that he is out. And if he is out, it must mean that you have a problem. The way forward is at the bottom of the bed. I am sorry that I have no other advice to give you. MM.

"She must mean there is something at the bottom of the bed that will help us," said Eddy. "So the first thing we need to do is find the bed."

74

Hen shone the torch round the room. The only thing large enough to be a bed lay under a faded dust sheet against one of the walls. Eddy and Hen took one corner of the dust sheet each, and pulled.

"Ooh!" Mitzee said. "Pretty!"

She was right. The bed that was under the dust sheet was very pretty. Its wooden frame was carved with animals and flowers, with details picked out in coloured glass beads. It was dressed with embroidered silk sheets that glowed purple and blue in the torchlight.

"Let's see what MM has left to help us," said Eddy.

Hen shone the torch at the foot of the bed, while Eddy ducked to look underneath and…

"There's nothing here," he said. "Nothing at all." He reached up and checked the underside of the bed frame. "And nothing hidden there either."

"Maybe it's on the bed itself," said Hen. "Perhaps there's a message in the carvings on the bottom panel."

They found that the carvings on the foot of the bed showed a family of monkeys chasing each other round a banana tree.

"I don't think that MM's message was to exercise and eat more fruit," said Eddy. "There must be something else."

"But if what we are looking for isn't under the bed, or part of the bed, where else is left?" said Hen.

"I can only think of one thing," said Eddy. "We haven't tried *in* the bed. Perhaps there's something tucked away down at the bottom." He dived under the silk covers and wriggled his way to the foot. He felt he had gone a long way before he reached the end of the mattress. He stuck his hands down to hunt for anything hidden there. But there was nothing.

"That's no good, either," he said. "I'm coming out."

But when he tried to turn round, he felt himself slipping forward, slithering over the smooth silk and out of the bottom end of the bed. As he fell he put his hands out, waiting to thump onto the floor.

But no thump came.

He carried on falling.

"Eddy?" Hen stared at the bed. A moment ago, there had been a big Eddy Stone-shaped bump in it. A bump that had suddenly disappeared.

"Eddy?" People didn't just vanish into thin air. That wasn't scientific at all. So where had he gone?

There was only one way to find out.

She clipped the torch to her belt, and slid head first into the bed after him.

Mitzee watched the glow of the torch moving under the silk sheets, towards the bottom of the bed. And then saw it disappear.

"I'm not staying here in the dark on my own," she said. "Wait for me. I'm coming after you!"

SHOES

As he fell from the bed, Eddy braced himself to meet the floor. He was still bracing himself when he realized that the floor wasn't coming. He opened his eyes just in time to see that he was heading for a big square of coloured cloth.

WHOOOOOMMMFFFF! He hit the cloth, slid down it, dropped another short distance, and landed with a CRUNCH on the gravel-covered ground. He lay there for a moment, catching his breath, then stood up very gingerly and discovered, to his delight, he hadn't broken any bones.

He looked around. The coloured square turned out to be the awning on a market stall, one of many that surrounded him.

He was just getting round to wondering where he was when he heard a WHOOOMMFFF! on a stall just to his left, and Hen flopped onto the ground.

"Where?" said Hen, looking wildly around her.

"No idea," said Eddy, helping her up.

"How?" said Hen, who was too surprised and confused even to try to put a sentence together.

"No," said Eddy. "Can't answer that one either."

"But…" said Hen, trying to manage more than one word at time. She didn't make it before there was another WHOOOMMFFF! as Mitzee touched down.

"Except," said Eddy, "MM's message said that the way forward was at the bottom of the bed. This must be what she meant – there was a gateway to…well, wherever this is. I think we must be in the country that MM visited. Where Wizard Witterwort came from."

"That's crazy," said Hen, pulling herself together. "You can't just fall out of bed and land somewhere completely different. It doesn't make any sense."

"I agree," said Eddy. "None at all. But we did it. Because, look – somewhere completely different is where we are." He helped Mitzee up.

"Ow!" Mitzee hopped from one foot to the other.

"Are you alright?" said Eddy.

"No," said Mitzee. "I need some proper shoes. These stones are going right through the stupid blue plastic bags on my feet."

"You could borrow my socks," said Eddy. "I can just wear my trainers."

"Your socks?" said Mitzee. "Off your feet? No thank you."

"I was just trying to help," said Eddy.

"Well try better! My toes are HURTING!!" Mitzee began to shout. "I NEED SHOES!!! PROPER SHOES!!! SOMEBODY FIND ME SOME SH— ooh, look, they're nice."

She pointed to a nearby stall that was stacked with pairs of silk slippers in every colour that you could think of.

"They are," said Eddy. "But this is a market. And we haven't got any money. So we can't buy anything."

"I am having a pair of those slippers," said Mitzee. "And if we haven't got money, I shall just use my good looks and charm."

"Charm?" said Hen. "Best of luck with that."

"Watch and learn, Babes," said Mitzee.

She picked her way over the gravel to the slipper stall.

A man was sitting next to it, crayoning a picture in a colouring book.

"You look like a kind man," said Mitzee. "Poor little me has lost her shoesies and now

CUTE CAMELS TO COLOUR IN

her toesies are getting all sore. Pleeeeeeeeeeaaase may I borrow one of your lovely pairs of slippers?"

"Stop messing about," the man said, barely looking up from his book. "Just take what you want."

Mitzee grabbed a pink pair and put them on.

"See," she said to Eddy and Hen. "It's easy when you know how. And are as pretty as I am."

"And behave like a little baby," said Hen. "Shoesies? Toesies? Ugh."

"I don't know about that," said Eddy. "The man on the stall doesn't seem to care what anyone does. Look."

They watched a woman walk up, take off the shoes she was wearing, and slip on a new green pair from the stall. Then she walked away, leaving her old shoes lying on the ground.

"There's something very odd about this market," said Eddy. "Excuse me," he called to the man on the stall. "That lady didn't pay. Aren't you bothered?"

"Why should I be bothered?" said the man. "This stall's nothing to do with me. I just like to sit here to do my colouring and watch the world go by. Anyway, what would she pay with?"

"Money?" said Eddy. "That's what people usually use."

"Money?" The man laughed. "You're not from round here, are you? I haven't seen any of that stuff since the Emperor took the throne, and decreed that everything was free."

"Free?" said Mitzee. "You mean *everything* everything? All of this?"

"That's right," said the man.

"I'm going to change out of this horrible white coat," she said. She headed off in the direction of a stall full of brightly coloured clothes.

"The Emperor," Eddy said to the man. "Would that be Gumpert the Glorious?"

"Blimey – you're way out of date. He's long gone. Now it's his son, Gumpert the Generous – long may he reign."

"So the Emperor gives you everything on these stalls?" said Eddy. "He must be fantastically rich."

"That's not it," said the man. "I mean, yes, he is fantastically rich. It is said that he blows his nose on sheets of gold. But it's his genie. Every day the Emperor tells the Genie to clear the city of all the old stuff that everyone has thrown away, and make new things for us to take. Food, clothes, useful household items, even knick-knacks, doodahs and thingummywotsits – you

name it, we get it for nothing. So no one
needs to work any more. We just sit
around all day finding ways to fill
in the time."

"And you do colouring in?"
said Hen.

"Not just colouring in,
obviously," said the man.
"That would be a
terrible waste of
the day. No.
Sometimes
I hum. Or
twiddle
my thumbs. I've
even been known to do
both at once, if I'm feeling very energetic."

"Here I come!" It was Mitzee. She was
wearing a long pale purple silk shirt,
a pair of baggy blue trousers, and had a
selection of pink and red scarves draped
round her neck. And she was carrying a
full bag in each hand.

"Take these, would you, Babes?" She tossed the bags at Eddy. "Just a couple of spare outfits. I'm not going to ask you how I look, because I already know. Fan-tas-tic. What are we doing now, then?"

"I'd like to know that, too," said Hen.

"I think we should start with the Emperor and his genie," said Eddy. "If it's the same genie who put the curse on Wizard Witterwort, we might be able to get him to take it off. Where will we find the Emperor?" he asked the man.

"In his palace of course. It's over there. Big thing. You can't miss it."

THE CODE

They didn't miss the palace.

They couldn't have missed it if they had tried. It stood behind a tall wall that shone in the sun like polished silver – mainly because it was made of polished silver. Over the top of that wall they could see a thicket of towers and spires and domes that bristled into the sky.

A great wooden door stood in the wall. Two men were sitting in front of it. They were wearing smart cream-coloured suits, and playing a game with coloured stones on a board.

"Excuse me," Eddy called to them. "We'd like to see the Emperor, please."

"I'm sure you would," said one of the men, without looking up from his game. "Question is, would the Emperor like to see you?"

"Have you got an invitation?" said the second man, moving one of the stones.

"No," said Eddy. "But…"

"Well, then, there's your answer," said the first man. "Off you go."

"Now what?" said Hen. "We'll never get over that wall. So if these guys won't open the gate for us, we're stuck."

"Go to the golden temple." Eddy jumped with surprise. The voice belonged to a figure who was standing beside him, where Eddy was sure a moment ago there had been no one at all. The figure was dressed from head to foot in a black robe, with a hood that hung over his head and completely shadowed his features, leaving only the two ends of a long curled moustache showing. "Five. Twenty-six. Forty-three. Finish," the man added.

He pointed to his left. Eddy turned, and saw that he was indicating a street that ran away from the corner of the palace wall.

When Eddy turned back, the figure had gone, as swiftly and silently as he had arrived.

"What was that?" said Hen.

"I don't know," said Eddy. "Except that it was a message. Two messages got us here – maybe this third one is telling us what we need to do now."

"And what about five, twenty-six, forty-three, finish? Do you think it's some sort of code?" said Hen.

"Could be," said Eddy. "Or a combination to open a door or a safe or something. If we can find this golden temple, then perhaps everything will be clear."

"It shouldn't be hard to spot," said Hen. "A golden temple doesn't sound like the sort of thing that you can hide."

But if it wasn't hiding, it was certainly doing a very good job of blending in. Eddy, Hen and Mitzee searched along the street that the stranger had pointed to. They found brightly painted houses, cafes with tables and chairs to soak up the sun, and shaded courtyards where fountains bubbled among fruit trees. All of it looked like it belonged in a holiday brochure, and none of it looked anything like a golden temple.

"We must have missed it," said Eddy.

"Or that stranger was just messing with us," said Hen.

"I'm going to find someone to ask," said Eddy.

"Well I need a rest," said Mitzee. "We've been walking for ages."

"There are some chairs over there," said Eddy, "in front of that cafe. Perhaps they wouldn't mind if you – wait a minute."

"I don't want to wait a minute," said Mitzee. "I want to sit down now."

"That's not what I meant," said Eddy. "Look what that sign says."

He pointed to a painted sign that was hanging in the front window of the cafe.

"I see it," said Hen. "And the letters say squiggle, squirl, sort of triangle with legs, and that last one looks a bit like an h that someone sat on."

"Oh, you can't read their alphabet, can you?" said Eddy. "Well I can't read anything else thanks to my wish, and what I can read on that sign is 'The Golden Temple Cafe'."

"You mean that's it?" said Hen. "That's what we've been looking for?"

"Let's go and find out," said Eddy.

The bell above the door clanged as he led the way into the cafe.

"Hello." A small round man with a shock of ginger hair and a bushy ginger beard stepped towards them. "Can I help you?" he asked in a husky voice.

"That depends," said Eddy. "What would you say if I said five, twenty-six, forty-three, finish?"

"I would say, excellent choice. Your food will be ready soon. Please take a seat." He turned and walked away.

"At last," said Mitzee. She plonked herself down on a chair.

"I think I've just ordered lunch," said Eddy. "Those numbers must be things that are on the menu."

"We don't want lunch," Hen called to the man. "We want to know the meaning of our code."

"What if this *is* the code?" said Eddy. "What if it means that if we eat the food, we'll find out what comes next."

"It doesn't sound very likely," said Hen. "But as I've already fallen out of the bottom of a bed and landed in a strange city where I'm sitting with a doll that has come to life and a boy who released a wizard and his curse, I think 'likely' is probably having a day off. And anyway, I'm hungry."

The waiter returned carrying a large metal tray. He put a jug of water and three glasses on the table, followed by three bowls of steaming liquid.

"Number five," he said. "Your starter. Soup of the day. And for this soup, the day was last Thursday."

The soup was thick and grey and had a smell that was part hot Labrador, part stagnant duck pond and altogether quite unpleasant.

"What's it made of?" Eddy asked. He wasn't sure he wanted to know.

"Leftovers," said the waiter.

"What sort of leftovers?" said Hen.

"Soup," said the waiter.

"So it's soup made from old soup?" said Eddy.

"Exactly," said the waiter.

"Babes, it looks lovely," Mitzee lied, "but could I just have an omelette and a green salad?"

"No," said the waiter.

Eddy dipped his spoon into the dingy liquid and took a cautious sip. The smell made him think that it would taste quite nasty, but it turned out that the smell was deceptive. It tasted very nasty.

"EUGHHHH!"

He put his spoon down again and took a large gulp of water.

"But what am I thinking?" said the waiter. "Stop! You must not eat this soup!"

Thank goodness, thought Eddy.

"I have forgotten the garnish," the waiter continued. He reached into his pocket and pulled out a handful of lumps of pale yellow fat, which he scattered into the three bowls.

"Now," said the waiter, "enjoy!" And he stomped back towards the kitchen.

Eddy looked at the soup. The fat had begun to melt, leaving an oily slick across its surface.

"I hate to say this," he said, "but the last word of the stranger's message was 'finish'. I think we have to eat it all if we want to find out what to do next."

It took a long time and many swigs of water to get through the bowl. It was quite the most horrible thing that Eddy had ever eaten.

And it remained the most horrible thing that Eddy had ever eaten for approximately two minutes after he had put his spoon down by the empty bowl.

Which is how long it took for the waiter to arrive with the next course.

TONGUE PUNISHMENT

"Number twenty-six," said the waiter. "Traditional pastries. An old peasant recipe from the old peasant village where my mother was an old peasant."

The pastries looked as large and lumpy as cobblestones. And about as appetizing.

Eddy attacked his with a knife and fork. The pastry won.

"They are usually eaten with fingers," said the waiter. "But the kitchen has run out of fingers so I have to serve yours with a vegetable instead." Then he let out a squeaky giggle. "That is a joke."

Unfortunately, the vegetable wasn't a joke. It was boiled celery. It sat steaming in its serving dish, pale and floppy. Eddy's least favourite vegetable of all. The big stick of tongue-punishment.

Eddy picked up the pastry and bit down on the hard crust. It crunched into pieces, and he took a mouthful of the filling. Cold, slimy jelly slithered over his tongue. The taste reminded him of old fish and vinegar and a hint of toothpaste. And not in a good way.

Groans came from either side as Hen and Mitzee did the same.

"BLEAH. And I thought the flavours Crispy invents were bad," said Hen. "Compared to this, even his egg and chutney potato twirls were delicious. And they were really horrid."

Eating was slow and miserable work. Every time Eddy took a bite of pastry, he just about managed to convince himself that a mouthful of celery would take the awful fishy taste away. And every time he swallowed a forkful of celery,

he just about managed to convince himself that
another chunk of pastry could only taste better.
Finally, he cleared his plate.

But before he had even had a moment to feel
satisfied that the main course was over, the waiter
was back.

"**Pudding time!**" he shouted. "Forty-three
– ice cream." He plonked down three tall glasses full
of the pale yellow dessert.

Maybe this won't be so bad, Eddy thought. *Surely
they can't make a mess of ice cream?*

But they could. It was sour, and cheesy, and as it
melted on his tongue it left behind bits of grit and
fluff that made his mouth
feel like he had been
licking out a Hoover bag.

But at last it was over. His spoon rattled in an empty glass. He took a huge gulp of water to wash all the bits of gunk off his teeth, and hoped that he wasn't going to be sick.

"You have finished," said the waiter. "And three courses, too. Most people only manage one. Well, that is a little fib. Most people don't even manage one. I think they are not used to our special spices and flavours. But you have done so well. So now, here is a little extra something."

"No more," said Eddy. "Please, don't make us eat anything else."

"It is not food," said the waiter.

"Neither was that lunch," said Hen with a groan.

The waiter pulled an envelope from his pocket and put it down in front of Mitzee.

"I give this to the prettiest at the table. It is another of our traditions. For you, lovely lady."

Mitzee opened the envelope.

"It's just squiggles," she said.

"Just squiggles to you," said Eddy.

"And just squiggles to you, too," said Mitzee. "Don't be rude."

"I mean," said Eddy, "it may not make sense to you, but I can probably understand it. Let me see."

He took the card and read out what was written on it.

Well, whoop de do! Would you flippin' believe it? You know what you've done? Course you don't. So, I'll tell you. You've only gone and got yourself an invitation to meet the grand gigglemaster himself, Emperor Gumpert the Generous. Is that the most brilliant thing you've ever heard, or what?

Fancy dress optional. Smile compulsory. So what are you waiting for? See ya at the palace!

"Do you think that invitation is genuine?" said Hen. "I thought an emperor would be more formal and serious."

"Maybe he is not dull and dreary like other emperors," said the waiter. "Maybe he is an all-round super guy and more fun than a sackful of squirrels. But what would I know about it, I am only a humble waiter in a traditional cafe."

"Well there's only one way to find out," said Eddy.

AN ALL-ROUND FUN GUY

"Follow me, please." The gatekeeper in the cream-coloured suit handed the invitation back to Mitzee. He was sounding a lot more polite than the last time they had met at the front of the palace. He pushed open the heavy gate, and led Eddy, Hen and Mitzee into the palace courtyard.

"Be careful how you go," he said, as they walked across the tiled floor towards a broad stone staircase.

"What do you mean?" said Eddy.

"Well, for starters," said the gatekeeper, "look out for the tripwire just below the first step."

"I see it," said Eddy. "What's it for?"

"In just a moment, sir. First, please hop over the fifth step. We don't want to set that one off."

"Set what off?" said Hen.

"The high pressure hosepipe, miss. The Emperor enjoys keeping us all on our toes. Now if you would like to follow me through here."

There was a grand archway at the top of the stairs. A heavy blue and gold curtain hung across it. The gatekeeper pushed the cloth to one side. They just had time to glimpse a dazzling room beyond, that was covered from floor to ceiling in beaten gold, when—

BANG!
SPLATTTTT!

A wodge of something white and sticky hit the gatekeeper full in the face.

"Oh," he said. "That's a new one."

"Are you okay?" said Eddy. "I think you're bleeding."

A thick trickle of red ran down from the gatekeeper's forehead, through the white mush and over his nose and mouth.

The gatekeeper stuck out his tongue and licked round his lips.

"Raspberry jam, I believe, sir. To go with the rice pudding. But thank you for your concern. Most kind."

"Ingenious," said Hen. She was holding up the bottom corner of the curtain. "A thread from here runs back to a little cannon just over there. One tug releases a pin that sets off a spring that pings a flint that makes a spark that lights the gunpowder and BANG."

"Not to mention splat, miss," the gatekeeper added.

"Ha ha!" A short round man wearing a swirly-patterned shirt, baggy red trousers and gold-coloured shoes studded with jewels bounced into view. A tall figure in hooded dark robes padded a few steps behind him. "I so got you!" the short round man said.

"Indeed, Majesty. Your Majesty so did get me," said the gatekeeper. "And most amusing it was." He didn't sound amused at all. "Permission to have a wash, Majesty."

"Yes, yes, run along. Now – Hello! Hello! Hello! to you three visitors. Come on in." He led the way into the golden room.

"And hello to you," said Eddy. "I'm sorry, I don't know what I should be calling you, but I guess you must be the Emperor?"

"That's me," said the Emperor. "And what you should be calling me is His Incredibly Imperial Majesty Gumpert the Generous, Wise Judge and Leader, Protector of His

People, Occupant of the Whopping Great Golden Throne, Lord of All He Surveys and a Heck of a Lot Further As Well, and All-Round Fun Guy. That's what it says on the door of the throne room. It's a very big door. But that's a bit formal. And long. Slows down conversation no end to have to keep saying it. So you can call me Bob."

"Bob?" said Eddy. "Why Bob?"

"Why not?" said the Emperor. "It's a good name. Short. To the point. Doesn't mess around. I've always liked it."

The hooded figure coughed quietly.

"Oh, yes," said the Emperor. "And this is my genie. The mighty Genie of the Baked Bean Tin."

"The Baked Bean Tin?" said Eddy. "I've never heard of a Genie of the Baked Bean Tin."

"Some genies get rings," said the Genie, in a booming voice. "Some get lamps. Some get other things. It's no big deal. I am Bimbambombadour, Maker of Miracles and Worker of Wonders, Commander of the Four Winds and the Seven Seas…"

"Blah, blah!" said the Emperor. "He goes on for hours like this if you let him. You can call him Bob, too."

"Won't that get confusing?" said Eddy.

"I do hope so," said the Emperor. "It might lead to all sorts of entertaining misunderstandings and mix-ups. In fact, to make it even more likely that we'll get in a complete muddle, I'm going to call you two Bob as well." He pointed at Eddy and Hen. "You on the other hand –" he looked at Mitzee – "I'm going to call absolutely gorgeous."

Mitzee said nothing, but giggled.

"Why would you want to get into a muddle?" said Eddy.

"Because, Bob, it's so boring when everything goes to plan," said the Emperor. "And thanks to Genie Bob here, everything always goes to plan. No matter how daft. I'll show you. O, Genie of the Baked Bean Tin."

"Yes, master," said the Genie. "What is your command?"

"Let's think – um – I want a chicken that lays bananas, a mint-flavoured hat and a small raincloud in that corner over there."

"Your wish, oh master, is my command – even if it is utterly stupid."

"Less of the chat, thank you," said the Emperor. "I may be the nicest master you've ever had, but that doesn't mean you can be cheeky."

The Genie spread out his arms and began to mutter under his breath.

"Are you the nicest master he's ever had?" said Hen.

"I'm certainly nicer than my dad, Gumpert the Glorious. It was all self, self, self with him. And grandad, Gumpert the Ghastly, was an absolute stinker. When I inherited the throne and the genie, I was determined to be nothing like them and to use the magic for the good of all the people. No one would want for food or clothes or a roof over their heads."

"Then this must be the happiest place in the world," said Hen.

"I like to think so, Bob," said the Emperor. "Although you should hear them complaining that today's shoes aren't quite the right shade of orange, or dinner's a bit too spicy, or they want a new house because the old one needs dusting."

The Genie clapped his hands. There was a brief flash on the Emperor's head as a wide floppy hat appeared. In the far corner of the room, a soft mist gathered itself into a small cloud, and started to rain on a chicken that was sitting on a silk cushion. The chicken looked up with a surprised expression, which turned to one of utter astonishment when it clucked and strained and laid a long yellow object.

"Banana, anyone?" said the Emperor, sucking the brim of his hat.

"I think I'll pass," said Eddy.

"So there you are," said the Emperor. "Three ridiculous things in an instant just because I ask for them. The hat's delicious, by the way, Bob."

"Thank you, master," said the Genie.

"Amazing," said Hen. "It's against all the rules of nature."

"And it gets so dull," said the Emperor. "Oh, it was great at first. Anything I wanted, any time. But after a while, it was just more and more stuff. I started to wonder what the point was. But when things get muddled up and go wrong, and when you play tricks on people and see how they react – well that's a different matter altogether. I never tire of it. Makes me laugh every time. Take your lunch for instance."

"How do you know about lunch?" said Eddy. "There was no one else there except the waiter."

"Oops!" said the Emperor. "Me and my big mouth." Eddy looked more closely at the short, round figure. He imagined him with a bushy ginger beard and wig.

"That was you," said Eddy. "You were the waiter."

"Guilty as charged," said the Emperor, in the husky voice he had used in the cafe. "You should have seen your faces when you had to eat the revolting muck that Bob here conjured up."

"You mean we had to swallow all that horrible – EUGH! –" the memory made Eddy feel ill – "just because you thought it was funny? What about how we felt?"

"Oh, come on, Bob," said the Emperor. "Where's your sense of humour? And as for all that stuff that's going on in Tidemark Bay, well you've got to admit that's an absolute hoot."

EVERYBODY NEEDS GOOD NEIGHBOURS

"You know about Tidemark Bay?" said Eddy.

"Of course," said the Emperor. "We've been watching."

"The statue of me that you took home," said the Genie. "It's a sort of transmitter. Like having eyes and ears all round the town. We gave it to Mad Monty when she took the lamp so we would be able to see if old Witterwort ever got out."

"And I just love what he's been up to," said the Emperor. "So funny."

"The whole town in a terrible mess?" said Eddy. "I don't think it's funny at all. That's why we're here. We want you to lift the curse and put everything back how it was."

"Is there something wrong with my ears?" the Emperor snapped. "You **do not** tell me what to do."

"You shouldn't frown like that," Mitzee said. "It makes you look twice as old and half as handsome. And you don't want that, do you, Babes?"

"No, of course," the Emperor stuttered, forcing his face back into a smile.

"That's better," said Mitzee. "Now, if you really want me to like you, you have to be nice."

"I suppose we've had our fun with Tidemark Bay," said the Emperor. "And if it will make you happy –" he smiled at Mitzee – "put it all back like it was, Bob."

"It's not quite so simple, master," said the Genie. "There is the matter of the curse."

"You put it on," said the Emperor, "so you can take it off, can't you?"

"Of course, master. But there are certain conditions. And it will take a while," said the Genie. "A while that we do not have. Your guest is almost here."

"I'd forgotten about him," said the Emperor. "We'll talk about Tidemark Bay tomorrow."

"Promise?" said Eddy.

"You don't ask me that. I am the Emperor. I said so

and I will."

"You're frowning again," said Mitzee. "Turn it upside down, please."

From somewhere outside the palace came a blast of trumpets.

"That's him," said the Emperor.

"Who?" said Hen.

"My neighbour, the Duke of Grimglower. Come and see," said the Emperor. He led the way across the golden room to windows that looked out over the palace walls.

A procession was making its way towards the entrance gate. Two burly trumpet players led a group of young women carrying baskets of deep purple rose petals that they were scattering on the ground. Behind them, six muscular men sweated to carry a padded chair slung between two stout poles. A thin figure dressed in a black suit and hat was seated in the chair. He was flanked by a dozen guards, who carried long spears with black pennants that hung limply in the still air.

"He's so full of himself," said the Emperor. "And so dull and miserable all the time. But we're going to have a little bit of fun with him, aren't we, Bob?"

"As we planned, master."

The Genie puffed out his cheeks and blew. A breeze began to flutter the pennants on the guards' spears. The rose petals that lay on the ground started to swirl and swoop, then formed into a whooshing whirlwind that whipped across the procession, sending the Duke's hat spinning into the sky and ripping the baskets from the young women's hands. More and more petals were sucked into the twisting column that soon rose as high as a house.

The Genie breathed a sound that was half sigh, and half roar. The seething spiral of petals shifted its shape into the form of a gigantic rearing snake, poised to strike the line of people below. The young women shrieked and threw themselves to the floor. The line of guards stood firm for a moment until the snake's head started to descend on them. Then they also shrieked and scattered. The bearers dropped the chair and the Duke tumbled onto the ground.

The Genie sucked in a deep breath. The wind died as quickly as it had risen, and a shower of rose petals fell through the air.

"Love the snake, Bob," the Emperor said with a laugh. "Now I must not be rude. Time to go and say hello."

The Duke was still being dusted down when the Emperor arrived at the front gate.

"Bit breezy today," the Emperor said cheerfully. "Come on in and have some tea. And there's no need for your guards. We're all friends here."

The Genie gave a wave, and the long spears that the guards were carrying drooped to the ground, their shafts turned to jelly and the blades to feathers.

Tea was a spectacular affair. The Genie conjured up fruits that burst in the mouth like honey bombs, delicately spiced cakes decorated with spun sugar that glinted like gold thread, and pots of creamy froth ripe with the taste of summer berries and the scent of sunlit orchards.

Eddy, Hen and Mitzee didn't feel like eating much after their revolting lunch. But they took a drink. The Duke had brought a delicious cordial flavoured with pineapple and ginger. It was a speciality of his homeland, he explained, insisting that everyone must taste it. And they all agreed that it was excellent.

After food came the entertainment. There were musical instruments that played themselves, brightly coloured birds that performed dizzying acrobatics in dazzling formations, and a dancing bolt of lightning – all the work of the Genie. The performance lasted long into the evening, and when it ended applause from everyone in the room rang long and loud. Even the Duke seemed to have softened a little after such lavish hospitality.

The Emperor turned to address him.

"My dear Duke, before we all retire to our beds for the night, I would like to present you with a gift – a token of the respect that I have for you."

From behind his chair he pulled out a silver casket as big as a cushion.

"You are too kind," the Duke said, taking the casket from him. He stood up so everyone could see and lifted the lid.

The spring mechanism was quick and powerful. By the

time anyone heard the BOING!!! the Duke's face was already full of the custard pie that it had flung at him.

The Emperor exploded in high-pitched giggles.

"Got you!" he shouted.

The Duke stood stock-still for a moment. Then without a sound he reached into a pocket and pulled out a large black handkerchief. He wiped the gunk first from his eyes, then from round his nose, and finally from over his mouth.

"HOO-HOO-HOO!" the Emperor hooted. He rolled off his chair and onto the floor, quivering with laughter.

"Your face! Oh, the look on your face!"

Eddy could see the look on the Duke's face. It chilled him to the bone.

SOMETHING GOES WRONG

That night, Eddy slept well.

The next morning, Eddy woke badly.

His head was thumping, and something noisy was happening in the street outside.

He went to the window and looked out over the market. A crowd of people were pointing at the palace walls and shouting. He couldn't tell what they were saying, but they didn't look happy.

He opened the window – then wished he hadn't. Voices banged against his eardrums. But he could hear words now. One woman was holding up a shoe and yelling, "This is muddy. I need a new pair. Why are there no shoes today?"

And a man was pointing at his shirt front and shouting, "I've lost a button. This shirt is ruined.

I want another one!"

What was going on? Eddy went to see if he could find out.

He found the Emperor slumped on a chair in the golden room, with Mitzee next to him.

"It's a calamity," said the Emperor. "When I woke up this morning that wretched Duke and all his people were gone. And the Genie and his baked bean tin were nowhere to be seen. The Duke must have stolen them in the night. My guards were out cold. It was that cordial that the Duke made sure everyone drank. I'm sure it was drugged."

"So that's why my head is sore," said Eddy. "Do you mean that the Duke is now the Genie's master?"

"No," said the Emperor. "The Genie gets back in his tin every night and seals the lid. You need the magic ring pull to get him out. And that's still safely on its chain round my neck. Without it the Duke will never open the tin. It's completely indestructible. So he can't command the Genie to do anything. But neither can I," he snuffled.

"There, there, Babes," said Mitzee. She patted his hand.

"What is all that row out there?" asked Hen, as she came into the room.

"It's the people," said the Emperor. "They are used to

getting stuff every morning. We had a lot of crackers in the palace larder left over from a party that will feed them for a day or two. But they want clothes and shoes and shiny things. And without the Genie, there won't be any more of those."

"What?" said Mitzee. "No more nice things ever?"

"None at all," said the Emperor. Mitzee stopped patting his hand.

"Can't you get the Genie back?" said Eddy. "The Duke can't have got far. If you send your best soldiers…"

"What soldiers?" said the Emperor. "We got rid of the army years ago. The Genie was all the protection we needed. But you're right. We need to gather people to go after him."

He went to the window and
flung it open.

"Listen to me," he shouted to the
crowd. The angry voices died down.

"For many years I have given you
all you have asked for. But today
I must ask for something
from you."

And then the BOOing started.

"In this moment of need…" the
Emperor went on.

"I'll tell
you about need!" a
voice yelled. "We need new socks!"

"We must stand together…"

"And cake!" yelled another voice. "Let us
eat cake!"

"What's happened to the Genie?" asked another.

And then a shoe flew through the air and whistled
past the Emperor's ear.

A barrage followed.

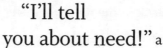

The Emperor stepped back and shut the window, as footwear pelted against it.

"They aren't going to help you," said Hen.

"So we'll have to," said Eddy. "We need the Genie to lift the curse and get Tidemark Bay back to normal. Are you with me, Hen?"

"Of course," said Hen.

"So the two of us…"

"Make that three, Babes," said Mitzee.

"But, gorgeous…" the Emperor began.

"Gorgeous nothing," said Mitzee. "I'm not stopping here if there are no new goodies. If we need the Genie to get them back on tap, then I'm in."

"Where will the Duke be going?" said Eddy.

"Back home to Grimglower Castle," said the Emperor. "It's north of here."

"Then that's where we're heading," said Eddy.

"You can't take the main road," said the Emperor. "I'm sure he'll leave guards posted along it. Luckily, there is another way."

"Don't tell me," said Eddy. "We can fly using the magic carpet that the Genie made for you."

"Magic what?" said the Emperor.

"Carpet," said Eddy. "They're in all the books."

"What a daft idea," said the Emperor. "How can you fly on a carpet? For a start there's nothing to hold on to. One quick turn and you'd be over the edge and hurtling to the ground. No, I can't see how that would work at all."

"Oh," said Eddy, rather disappointed. "So what is the other way?"

"The desert road," said the Emperor. "They'll never expect you to use that."

"Why not?" said Hen.

"Because it's so dan— neglected."

"Were you going to say dangerous?" said Eddy.

"There are one or two tricky bits. The Whispering Sands, for instance."

"And what happens there?"

"They whisper," said the Emperor.

"That doesn't sound too bad," said Eddy.

"And there are a few birds to look out for."

"What sort of birds?"

"You'll know when you see one," said the Emperor. "I can't give you a jet-propelled bath mat or anything like that. But I can give you a plan of Grimglower

119

Castle to help you to find your way round. And lots of crackers and water. You'd better take a donkey to carry the supplies. There is a fellow down in the market who will sort you out. Good luck."

He only just managed to stop himself from adding, "You'll need it."

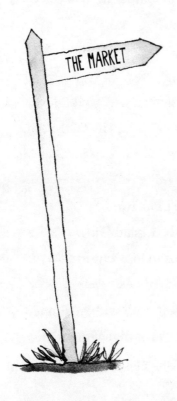

TRANSPORT PROBLEMS

"No. No donkeys today." The man in the market shook his head.

"It's for a job for the Emperor," said Eddy.

"Especially not for the Emperor," said the man.

"But you've got loads of donkeys just sitting around," said Eddy. "A whole big herd."

"Or is it a flock?" said Mitzee.

"Today it is a strike," said the man. "A whole big strike of donkeys. I had to eat dry crackers for breakfast, instead of honey and fruit. No breakfast, no donkey."

"There won't be any breakfast tomorrow either unless we get the Genie back," said Eddy, "and we can't do that without help to carry our supplies."

"So really, it's no donkey, no breakfast," Hen joined in.

"Hmm." The man thought for a moment. "I tell you what. You may have a camel. That camel." He pointed over to where all his animals were tethered. There were a dozen camels. The one he was pointing at was sitting in a small pen of its own.

"Why that one?" said Eddy.

"Because if you never come back and I lose that useless beast, it is no matter," said the man. And with that he turned and walked away.

"I wonder why he picked this one," said Eddy. "It doesn't look any worse than the others."

"They aren't your favourite animals, then?" said Hen.

"They're smelly and grumpy and they look like they were designed as a joke," said Eddy. "What's to like?"

"I think they're quite sweet," said Hen. She held out her hand to the lone camel. "Aren't you?"

The camel looked up at her and let out a loud dribbly belch. A smell wafted through the air, like something that was lurking at the bottom of a bin long after it should have gone to the rubbish tip.

"How do you think we get him to stand up?" said Eddy.

"I don't know," said Hen. "I'm better with machines. They have knobs and switches to make them do things. Come on, camel, up you get." She waved her arms in encouragement.

"HUP!" Eddy demonstrated by jumping in the air. "HUP! HUP!"

The camel stared back at them. The camel slowly chewed a mouthful of hay. The camel did not hup.

"I don't suppose that one of your outfits was a zookeeper, was it?" Eddy said to Mitzee. "A zookeeper would know what to do."

"Far too smelly for me," said Mitzee. "I had a pony but he never sat down because he didn't have bendy knees."

"Wait a minute," said Hen. "The camel's got something stuck in his ears. Maybe he just can't hear us." She looked more closely, and pulled a big ball of cotton wool out of each hairy ear. "Can you get up, please?" she asked quietly.

"Oh, I see," said the camel, in a drawling voice. "So that's what all the jumping and waving was about. I thought you must be part of some travelling dance show."

He gave another chew.

"No," said Eddy. "We're not dancers."

"Good job," said the camel. "You were terrible."

"We need you to go on a journey with us," said Eddy. "So – um, sorry, do you have a name?"

"Claudius," said the camel.

"So, Claudius, would it be too much trouble to stand up, like we're asking?"

"That depends," said Claudius. "On what you mean by too much."

Hen laughed.

"What's funny?" said Eddy.

"This," said Hen. "When I got up this morning, I knew how things worked. Forces and actions and reactions. It all made sense. Nice and logical. And now we're wondering what to do with a talking camel."

"I bet it was the Genie who made you speak," said Eddy.

"That's right," said Claudius. "The Emperor thought

it would be amusing. We can all talk now. Isn't that right, chaps?" he called to the other camels.

"When there's something worth saying," one called back.

And that was the end of that conversation.

"The Genie has been stolen," said Eddy, "and we need you to help us to steal him back."

"Well, why didn't you say so?" said Claudius. "He's a good fellow, that Genie. Stand clear, one is going for vertical."

Moving with all the grace of a cow on an ice rink, he kneeled up halfway on his front legs, shoved his bottom into the air with his back legs, and then staggered and stumbled upright.

"How do we get on your back?" said Hen. She looked up at Claudius, who now towered above her. "Are there some steps somewhere?"

"You have to get on," said Claudius, "before I get up. And if you are going to ask if it's too much trouble for me to get back down again, don't bother, because yes it is. You'll just have walk for now."

"Walk?" said Mitzee. "In these shoes?"

"At least you can carry these water bottles and bags

of crackers," said Eddy, as he and Hen attached them
to straps on the camel's harness.

"And my spare clothes," said Mitzee, adding her
two large bags. "In case I need to change outfits.
What's the dress code for stealing? Party frock?
Business suit? High heels or sandals?"

The group headed out of the city towards the road
to the north. They came to a small square, where
people were sitting and grumbling about the lack of
goodies while passing the time as usual. One woman

was painting a portrait of a young girl. Two men were laying out a game of draughts. And with a clatter of castanets, a small band of musicians struck up a sprightly tune.

"Oh, dear," said Claudius.

"Something wrong?" said Eddy. He noticed that the camel was starting to nod his head in time to the music.

"Oh, goodness," said Claudius. The nodding got wilder.

"I advise you to keep back." His legs started to twitch. "One simply has to DANCE!" he yelled.

His bottom rocked from side to side
and he suddenly exploded into wild
gyrations. He spun round and round,
his feet kicking out at crazy angles. Paint
pots, draughts, water bottles, chairs and
tables flew through the air and clattered
to the ground as Typhoon Claudius
whirled out of control. Everyone
dived frantically out of the way.

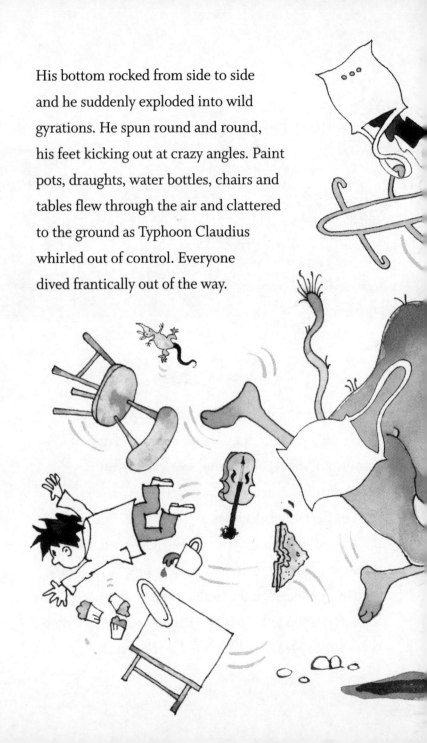

"Stop the band!" Claudius shouted as he twisted and twirled, "Stop the band!"

But no one needed to stop them. In the face of the flurry of flailing legs, they stopped themselves and ran for cover.

Claudius collapsed in a panting heap.

"Are you alright?" A grey-haired man who was wearing a tattered old smock lifted Eddy off the ground, and dusted him down.

"A few bruises," said Eddy, catching his breath, "but nothing serious, thanks."

"I do apologize," the camel groaned. He staggered back to his feet. "I simply can't help it. It's those castanets. Once those little bits of wood start clicking they set my whole body shaking and I lose control."

"So that's why your ears were stuffed up," said Eddy.

"And why your owner was happy to let you go," said Hen.

"I got into a bit of bother when I made a mess of one of the Emperor's parades," said Claudius. "I've been in disgrace ever since."

"There doesn't seem to be any real harm done," said Eddy, picking up one of the water bottles. Around

130

the square, people were putting things back in order. "But has anyone seen the plan of Grimglower Castle that the Emperor gave me? It was tucked into my belt."

They hunted round. But it was nowhere to be seen.

Eddy had a sudden thought that made his stomach turn over.

"That man who helped me up," he said. "He must have taken it when he brushed the dust off me. We've got to get it back. We'll never find our way through the castle without it."

THE
GANG

Eddy yelled across the square. "Did anyone see where the man with grey hair went?"

"That way!" a girl answered, pointing down a dim and narrow alley with high windowless walls on each side. Eddy and Hen set off after him. They turned a sharp corner and ran smack into a dead end.

"He can't have come this way," said Hen. "We haven't passed anywhere that he could have turned off. That girl must have been mistaken."

"Unless—" said Eddy.

"Don't tell me," said Hen. "Unless he suddenly became invisible or sprouted wings and flew away or some other unscientific thing that makes no sense at all."

"No," said Eddy. "Think about it. Why would anyone build an alley that doesn't go anywhere?"

"Maybe it just got blocked off," said Hen.

"Or maybe it just looks like it," said Eddy. He ran his fingers over the wall, examining it closely. "There's a metal plate here. It's really grimy – looks like it hasn't been cleaned for years." He rubbed at the dirt with his sleeve. "There are letters underneath the grunge. Let's see – it says:

'*Den of the Forty Thieves. Knock twice, then go away. We're not interested. We didn't take it. We weren't even there.*'"

"There's a big crack in the wall between those two stones," said Hen. "And look – it runs up in a line and across and down again to the ground over there. Just like a hidden door."

"So that's where our thief went," said Eddy.

"I wonder how you open it," said Hen.

"If this was like in stories, we'd just have to say Open Sesame!" said Eddy. There was a low, grumbling, grating noise. The wall in front of them began to shake, and then swung backwards.

They were surprised to find
themselves staring at four men
who were sitting on stools in a vast
and almost empty space.

The four men appeared equally
surprised to find themselves
being stared at.

"How did you do that?" one of them said.

"I just said Open Sesame," said Eddy.

"What did I tell you?" said the man. "Didn't I say we should change that password? Didn't I say it wasn't secure enough?"

Eddy noticed one of the others, a grey-haired man, slip something into the sleeve of the smock he was wearing.

"I think you have something that belongs to me," said Eddy.

"Don't think so," said the grey-haired man.

"What was that, then, that you just hid up your sleeve?"

"I didn't hide anything."

"Then show me," said Eddy.

The man spread out his arms to show that he had nothing hidden up his sleeve. And the thing that he had hidden up his sleeve fell out onto the floor. It was a roll of paper, the same size and colour as the one that Eddy had been carrying.

"Call that nothing?" said Eddy, pointing at it.

"What, that?" said the man. "Oh, that – um…" He hesitated. And…

"…we got it off a bloke in a bazaar…"

"…it's my shopping list…"

"…a cardboard telescope…" the other three chimed in at once.

"Alright," said the grey-haired man. "It's true. I took it from you in the square."

He picked it up and handed it back to Eddy.

"I didn't mean any harm. Just practice. Keeping the old fingers in shape."

"You're thieves, then," said Eddy. "Like it says on the door. But aren't there supposed to be forty of you? And shouldn't this place be full of your loot? Stacks of gold, pearls as big as conkers, diamonds as big as gulls' eggs, and emeralds as big as very fat hamsters."

"We've dwindled," said the grey-haired man. "What's the point of thieving, or keeping a stash of loot, when everyone can get anything they want for free any day of the week?"

"It's just the four of us now," said another. "Six, there," he pointed to the grey-haired man, "Nineteen and Twenty-three over here," he pointed to the other two, "and I'm Thirty-one."

"It's more of a social club than a gang now," said Twenty-three. "A few games of dominoes, and a chat about the old days over a cup of tea. That's what keeps us going."

"The old skills are dying out," said Six. "Which is why I'm determined to keep mine up, even if there aren't any proper thieving jobs to be had any more."

"How would you like a proper job?" said Eddy. "A really big one?"

"Proper?" said Nineteen. "You mean, like pinching something and not having to give it back afterwards?"

"This one's definitely for keeps," said Eddy. "We're going to break into Grimglower Castle and get the Genie of the Baked Bean Tin back."

"That is a proper job," said Six. "And from the look of those plans of the castle, it's a proper challenge and all. What do you say, lads? One last big job for us to go out on?"

"I'm in."

"Me too."

"And me."

"Right," said Six. "The old gang's back in action. What's left of us, anyway. I never thought I'd see the day. I'm going to get all emotional in a minute. When do we start?"

"Right now," said Eddy.

THE ROAD TO GRIMGLOWER

It was hot.

Really hot.

Hot enough to cook your lunch by cracking an egg and frying it on the rocks at the side of the path.

Although soup would have been a bit of a challenge.

They had been walking for hours. All except Mitzee, who managed ten minutes and then started complaining that her feet hurt. She carried on complaining so loudly that it was soon decided that if she would just keep quiet, she could ride on Claudius. Everyone agreed. Even Claudius.

The journey had taken them through a dense wood and across lush green fields. But the further they went, the drier the land became, and now they were standing on a parched hill and looking down on a pale brown desert that stretched away to the horizon.

They stopped for a moment to take a mouthful of water.

"I guess," said Eddy, "those must be the Whispering Sands."

He heard a spluttering behind him, as Thirty-one choked on his drink.

"No one said anything about the Whispering Sands when we agreed to come on this trip," said Thirty-one, still coughing. "Are you seriously suggesting that we try to cross them?"

"Is there a problem?" said Eddy.

"Are you bonkers?" said Twenty-three.

"If he isn't now, he soon will be," said Nineteen. "Do you know what happens out there?"

"No," said Eddy. "What?"

"Well, I don't know either," said Nineteen. "On account of how anybody who has ever managed to get across is a gibbering, blibbering wreck by the time they get to the other side."

"And they're the lucky ones," said Thirty-one. "Most people who try to cross are never seen again."

"That's just traveller's tales," said Six. "Wild stories."

"Tell that to my brother," said Nineteen. "By the time he got across he thought he was a piece of cheese. Used to sleep between two slices of bread. Then he started to go mouldy. The smell got so bad that we had to get him to live outside in a tent."

"There's no way I'm going into those sands," said Twenty-three.

"Nor me," said Thirty-one.

"What about the gang getting together again?" said Six. "We agreed to help these people."

"We can still be together," said Nineteen. "We three are going back. And if you've got any sense, you will too."

"I'm stopping," said Six.

"Then I hope we'll see you again soon," said Twenty-three. "Safe and sane."

"Sorry," said Thirty-one. "But…you know." He shrugged his shoulders, picked up his bottle of water, and led Nineteen and Twenty-three back the way they had come.

The others stood silently for a moment, watching them go.

"Time to get moving," said Eddy.

He led the way into the tall sand dunes that lay ahead of them. A breeze whirled round their ankles, blowing drifts of sand through the clear, bright air. It was stronger at the top of the dunes, where it whipped against their faces, and whistled in their ears.

"Do you think that noise is the whispering?" said Hen.

"If that's all we have to put up with, it won't be so bad," said Eddy.

They tramped onwards, over dune after dune.

WhhhhhiSSSSSShhhhh
SssssSWWWWiSSSSSShhhhhh

The wind whooshed around them.

Shhhhhould have turned back

Eddy could have sworn that he heard the words in his ear.

"Who said that?" said Six.

"Did you hear it, too?" said Hen.

Shhhhhould never have come
Sssssstill time to turn round

A chorus of voices slithered into Eddy's ear, twining and winding their way right into his brain.

Sssssstill time to sssssave yourselves

"Do you think we should go back to the others?" said Six.

"No," said Eddy. "We need to press on. Come on, up this next dune."

Whhhhhy presssss on?
Whhhhhat'ssssss the point?
Whhhhhen you can't sssssucccccceed?

"Of course we can succeed," said Eddy. "We've got Six with us. He's a proper thief."

Sssssixxxxx?
Sssss...sssss...sssss

It sounded like they were laughing. Mocking.

Sssssixxxxx isssss uselessss
Uselessss and ollllld

"They've got a point," said Six. "It's years since I did any proper thieving."

Whhhhat about the casssstle guardssss?
With their shhhhharp sssssswordsssss?

"We haven't thought about the guards and what happens when we get to the castle," said Hen. "We haven't really got a plan at all, have we?"

"We'll work something out," said Eddy. "Probably."

The voices were picking at his doubts, speaking aloud all the worries that he was trying to keep in check. And his confidence was unravelling like an old scarf snagged on barbed wire.

"I don't think we can do this," said Six.

Ssssstupid to try
Sssssilly to go on
Sssssenssssssible to ssssstop

"The Emperor should be sorting this out," said Hen. "Not us."

"Maybe we should go back," said Eddy. "I haven't really thought this through."

Whhhhhichhhhh way is back?
Whhhhhichhhhh way?
Whhhhhichhhhh way?

"We can follow our footsteps," said Eddy, turning to look behind him. But the wind had wiped them clean.

They were in the middle of a great ocean of sand. He couldn't be sure any more which way they had come. Or, when he turned back round, which way they were going.

"We should have brought a compass," he said.

No compasssss
Sssssilly
Shhhhhould have a compasssss

"I think it's that way," said Six, pointing to the left.
"No, no, it's this way," said Eddy, pointing to the right.

Lossssst
Lossssst
Walking in circlesssss

"Have we been walking round in circles?" said Hen.

"I don't know," said Eddy. "I don't know anything any more. But we've got Claudius. Camels know how to find their way in a desert, don't they?"

"Don't ask me," said Claudius. "I would have brought a compass."

Circlesssss
Till they run out of water
And thhhhhen

The voices didn't need to say any more. Everyone knew very well what would happen if they ran out of water while they were lost in the desert.

BEIGE IS <u>NOT</u> A COLOUR

It's all my fault, Eddy thought. *From buying that head to breaking the lamp to getting us lost in this desert. All my stupid fault.*

Sssss
Sssss
Sssss

The Whispering Sands hissed with laughter.

Round in circlessssss
Lossssst
Never find the way

"Yeah, we will. No probs," Mitzee said. She was sitting on the camel, on top of the next dune. "I can see a big castle up ahead in the distance."

There'sssss nothing there
It's jussssst an illusion
Jussssst a mirage

"I don't even know what one of those is, alright?" said Mitzee, "but I do know…"

Oh, for goodnesssss' sssssake

One of the whispering voices spoke alone.
It sounded impatient.

A mirage is a displaced image of a distant object

"Excuse me," said Mitzee. "I was talking and it's very rude to interrupt. And I know what I can see."

It's not really there. It's the hot air making the light refract

"What sort of a word is that?" said Mitzee. "Refract. I've never heard of it."

That doesn't surprise me

"And what's **that** supposed to mean?"

Not very bright, are you? Just an airhead

"Airhead? That's good, coming from something who is air all over."

Sssss...sssss...sssss

One of the other whispering voices laughed.

Are you laughing at what she said? the first whispering voice asked.

It was quite funny, said the second.

You're not doing the whoooossshh thing. The whhh and the shhhh, said the third whisperer.

Never mind the whoooossshh thing, said the first whisperer. You were laughing at me

You've got to do the whoooooosssh thing, said the third whisperer. That's what makes us sound sinister

You were laughing, said the first whisperer. How sinister is that? Laughing at what this airhead in the tasteless clothes said

"Tasteless?" said Mitzee. "Lavender with orange is totally on trend, thank you very much. I've done interior design and colour matching, so there. And who are you to talk about colour anyway? Just look at this desert."

What do you mean? said the first whisperer.

"It's beige everywhere. Boring, boring, boring. Beige isn't a colour – it's an excuse."

There was a sudden snort of wind.

Are you laughing now, too? the first whisperer said grumpily.

Well it was funny, said another.

No it wasn't. It was just rude

Oh come on, admit it. Beige is a bit dull

You're agreeing with her now? We're meant to destroy her confidence and leave her a shivering wreck

We were doing alright until you started showing off. Displaced. Refract. What's all the fancy language for?

Yeah, what's wrong with a good whhooooShhhh?

Another whisperer joined the argument.

Oh, don't you start. At least I was putting some effort in

And they drifted away over the sand, squabbling together instead of tormenting the travellers. And as the voices faded, all the doubts that had built up didn't seem quite so bad any more.

"You know," said Eddy. "This desert isn't so big."

"You know," said Hen. "I can make us a compass. I've got a magnet and a needle in my tool bag. If I magnetize the needle, we can attach it to a cork from one of the water bottles, float it on a cup of water, and it will point north. I'll get on with it."

"You know," said Six. "With my thieving experience, I'm sure I can get us into the palace to steal that Genie."

"You did well," Eddy said to Mitzee.

"Yes," said Hen. "Those voices really got to all of us. Except you. How did you manage that?"

"Simple, Babes. When you know you're right, you can just ignore anyone who disagrees with you. And I'm always right. I call it mind over matter. I don't mind what they say, because it doesn't matter."

"Yes, I can see how that would do it," said Hen, as she finished making the compass. "The needle is showing that north is this way," she pointed. "Let's go."

After a couple of hours they came to the far edge of the desert. They were dusty, hot and tired. But safe.

Now they could all see Grimglower Castle in the distance. And this was no mirage. Huge and black, it loomed over the land around it. It stood on a hill, across a broad plain that was strewn with boulders and large stones, and bordered on either side by craggy mountains.

"I reckon we can be there by the end of the afternoon," said Eddy. "Let's take a break for lunch."

They unloaded their bags of crackers and bottles of water, and sat by the side of a pile of boulders as they ate.

"I am going to have a beauty nap," said Mitzee. She settled in a sunny spot and closed her eyes.

A bird of the small brown variety hopped across the ground nearby looking for stray crumbs.

"That reminds me," said Eddy. "The Emperor said we had to look out for some birds."

"What sort of birds?" said Six.

"He just said we'd know when we saw one," said Hen.

"I think I know now," said Six. He was pointing at the sky.

Eddy and Hen looked up. A shape like a jumbo jet was

flying low towards
them, but a jumbo jet with
feathered wings and a
hooked beak where its
nose cone should be.
As it came
nearer, its huge
shadow fell across them.
"Where did the sun go?"
said Mitzee, without
opening her eyes.

"Oh – my – gosh," said Eddy,
standing up, as Hen scrambled to her feet beside him.
The shape was getting bigger with every second. Not
just getting nearer, Eddy realized with a jolt, but getting
lower. He could see its legs stretched out and a set of long
curved talons glinting on each foot. Talons that were big
enough to hook an elephant – sharp and
open and coming straight at them.

UN-OKAY

"Look out!" shouted Six. He dived behind the pile
of boulders, with Claudius close behind him.

Eddy and Hen stood frozen to the spot. Eddy wanted
to run away, but the messages from his brain to his legs
were getting mixed up. Instead of rushing him to safety,
his limbs were putting all their energy into trembling
like jelly.

The massive bird swooped down on them. Eddy
stared in horror at the talons that were spearing
towards him. And still his legs refused to run.

Suddenly he was lifted off his feet. The talons had
closed around him like a cage, without even scratching
him. But now he was trapped as securely as if he were
behind thick iron bars.

"Let go!" he shouted, as the bird beat its wings, making a draught that scattered the travellers' lunch across the plain, and blew Mitzee's hair out of shape.

"What's going on?" she said sitting up and seeing the mess around her.

"Put me down!" Eddy yelled again. "Let go!"

The great wings beat once more, and in an instant they were high in the air. The ground was a very long way down.

"I've changed my mind!" shouted Eddy. "Don't let go! Please don't let go!"

He peered out between the bird's talons. Ahead of him he could see the mountain range that stood at the edge of the plain. He looked around – and saw Hen trapped inside the bird's other foot. Her eyes were wide open in shock. Her mouth was moving, but if she was speaking he couldn't hear her over the rush of air as the bird sped on.

They were getting close to the mountains now, flying towards a jagged spike of rock. Clinging to the top of the spike was an immense tree. Its branches opened out into a massive bowl, and as they got near Eddy could see that the bowl was cluttered with smaller tree trunks and thick pieces of wood that had been bent and woven together to form a colossal nest.

The bird spread its wings to brake and dropped Eddy and Hen on one side of the nest. The impact forced the air out of Eddy's body. It would have broken his bones if the bottom of the nest had not been lined with softer material – giant leaves, and animal skins, and enormous feathers.

"Are you okay?" he asked Hen, gasping to get his breath back.

"Don't be ridiculous," she said. "We're stuck way up in the air in the nest of a giant bird. This is about as un-okay as I've ever been in my life. And I think it's about to get worse. Look."

The bird looped round in the air, and landed in the middle of the nest, eyeing them. It pushed its head close. Its beak was easily big enough to swallow either one of them whole.

Or both of them, if it chewed.

Moments earlier, they had been enjoying a quiet lunch. Now it looked they were going to *be* lunch.

But the bird turned, hopped off the edge of the nest, and spread its wings and flapped away.

"Thank goodness," said Eddy. "I thought it was going to eat us."

"It's probably just saving us for later," said Hen. "Let's face it, I don't think it brought us back here because it was lonely and wanted some company. So what do we do now?"

"I don't know," said Eddy. "Let's take a look around."

There wasn't much to see. The nest was as broad and as deep as a swimming pool. Apart from them, the only things on the floor in the middle were some heaps of sun-bleached bones, and a large, white, oval boulder.

"What do you think that boulder is doing up here?" said Hen.

They went to take a closer look.

"Not much," said Eddy. "Which I suppose is what you would expect a boulder to do. Hang on though. What's that knocking?"

A hollow thumping noise started to echo round the nest, like someone repeatedly driving a steamroller into the face of a cliff.

"I think it's coming from inside the boulder," said Hen.

There was a sudden loud CRUNCH, like a thousand sets of teeth biting down on a thousand slices of crisp toast.

And then a crack opened up on the boulder.

The end of something sharp poked out.

"I don't think this is a boulder," said Eddy. "I think it's an egg. And I think it's hatching. And I think that we've been delivered to be Junior's first meal. We need to get out of here. Now."

"I agree," said Hen. "With everything you've just said – especially the getting-out-of-here part. The problem is – how?"

NOTHING WORKS

Eddy picked his way towards the edge of the nest. He tested every step as he went, carefully making sure that the floor was solid beneath its covering of leaves and fur and feathers.

And as he got nearer to the edge he had to be just as careful to avoid great heaps of bird droppings that were all around, some dried as hard as concrete by the sun, and some still sticky and stinky.

At the outer rim he faced a wall of tangled branches that came up to his waist. He found a foothold on a sturdy branch, and hauled himself up onto the top of the rim.

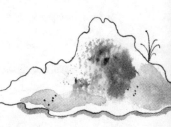

"Be careful," said Hen, who was following close behind him.

"Don't worry," said Eddy. "I just want to see if there's any way down from here."

He crawled out on the rim. Sharp points of wood dug into his hands and knees as he moved forward. He stuck his head out over the edge of the nest – and immediately wished he hadn't. The view sent a wave of dizziness rippling through him.

"Wow," he said. "It really is a very, very long way to the bottom."

"Do you think we could climb down?" said Hen.

"I don't know," said Eddy. "We'd have to go over the side here, then hold on and swing by our arms to get across the underside of the nest until we reached the trunk of the tree. It would be like doing monkey bars in the gym. How are you at those?"

"Not great," said Hen. "I don't know how long I'd be able to hang on."

"No," said Eddy. "Neither do I. If we had a really long piece of rope we might be able to lower ourselves over the edge."

"I've got a big ball of string in here," said Hen,

pointing to the tool bag that was slung from her belt. "But it's not long enough or strong enough for that."

"I don't think this way is going to work," said Eddy. "I'm coming back."

He shuffled backwards, and dropped onto the floor.

At that moment there was a cracking, crunching noise from behind him, and a chunk of eggshell, as big and thick as a dinner plate, flew past his shoulder. When he turned round he could see the chick's eye staring out of the egg at them through the hole its beak had just made. It reminded him of the way the big dog that lived up the road from him looked at sausages.

"We've got to do something," said Hen. "That bird isn't going to be stuck in there much longer. Maybe we could go down through the middle of the nest and straight onto the tree."

"That sounds worth a try," said Eddy. "Let's pick a spot over there. We'll just need to shift all the feathers and leaves, and then we can see if we can find a way through."

Just shifting turned out to be a lot harder than expected. The leaves were okay, but the feathers were awkward. They weren't heavy, but most of them were twice as long as Eddy was tall, and just moving them through the air felt like trying to push a brick through a tub of treacle.

They were both panting by the time they had cleared a spot. They looked down at the tangle of thick branches that formed the floor of the nest.

"You'd have to be a snake to wriggle through that lot," said Eddy. "We're going to have to make a gap." He tugged at a branch. It didn't move.

He strained and grunted and heaved.

It still didn't move.

"It's woven together really tightly," he said. "Do you think we could cut our way through? Have you got a saw in your toolbag?"

"Of course," said Hen. "But not one that's going to do this job for us." She pulled out a folding saw. Its blade was just about as long as her finger. Her little finger.

"Useful for lots of things, but it will never

get through all that wood. So that's another idea that won't work," said Hen. "We've got about as much chance of flying away."

Flying.

That reminded Eddy of something.

What was it?

And then it came to him in a flash like a light being turned on in his head.

"Okay," he said. "I've got an idea of how to get out of here. Maybe. Stop me if this sounds completely crazy."

EDDY GETS HIS HANDS DIRTY

"Stop you if it sounds crazy?" said Hen. "You mean crazier that being stranded in the nest of a giant bird whose chick is about to hatch out and eat us for lunch? This idea of yours would have to be completely bonkers to beat that."

"Well," said Eddy, "it might just be. I've remembered something. I've got a book at home. It's about here. There's a picture in it that didn't mean much when I saw it. But now, I think it might be showing us how to escape."

"Go on," said Hen. "This all sounds unlikely, but it hasn't reached crazy yet."

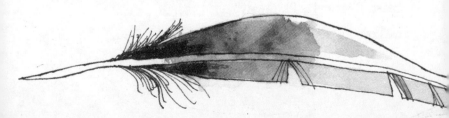

"In the picture there's a very tall tree, and a man jumping out of it with wings on his back. These big feathers lying around…"

"BONG!" said Hen. "And stop. People can't fly. We haven't got big enough arm muscles. I've seen videos of birdmen jumping off things. They all go the same way. Flap, flap, splat. We would be just the same if we tried it. Except, in our case there would be a very long gap between flap and splat because we've got a very long way to fall."

"Not flying," said Eddy. "Gliding. You're an engineer – do you think that a couple of these big feathers would give enough lift for one of us to glide safely down to the ground?"

"I suppose they might," said Hen. "In theory. But we would never be able to hold them and keep our arms out straight. Like I said, our muscles aren't big enough."

"So we fasten the feathers on with something," said Eddy. "You've got string."

"String's too weak," said Hen. "They would be ripped apart. But hey! – I know what we could use."

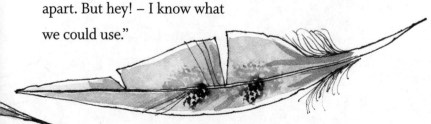

Hen continued, "There are loads of animal skins lying round here. If we cut those into strips and knot them together they will be as good as ropes. And my little saw is sharp enough to cut a couple of straight pieces of wood to go across our shoulders. So we find two matching pairs of feathers – left and right – strap those onto the wood and tie the whole thing over our shoulders. If we're very lucky, that could work."

"Then what are we waiting for?" said Eddy.

"Who's waiting?" said Hen. She was already sawing at a branch.

They worked fast. In just a few minutes they had gathered their materials together.

In those same few minutes, the chick had battered a hole in the eggshell large enough to stick its beak through, and was now chomping away to free itself.

Eddy laid two feathers quill to quill across each piece of wood. Hen wound the skin ropes round and round the smooth ends, binding them to the support, while Eddy held them in place.

Hen finished the second one and tied it off, leaving two long trailing ends of rope.

"I think that's it," she said. "Let's see if it's going to hold."

They lifted one of the sets of wings off the floor. The feathers shifted in the ropes as the fastenings took their weight.

"It's no good," she said. "They aren't firm enough. They won't hold up in flight."

"What can we do?" said Eddy. He looked across at the egg. The chick's whole head was now poking free. "Whatever it is, we need to be quick."

"If only we had some really strong glue," said Hen. "A layer of that and then some more skin ropes on top would do the job."

"If you need sticky stuff," said Eddy, "there's masses of it lying around here." He took a deep breath, stepped over to a big wet pile of bird droppings, plunged his hands into it and scooped a load up. It was thick, and gungy, and about as horrible and smelly as he had expected.

He slapped it across the bindings on the first set of wings.

"There. You tie them up while I get some more for the other ones."

If we get out of this, I really must remember to wash my hands before tea, he thought, as he plastered another load of the foul-smelling goo onto the second set of wings.

He watched the chick while Hen worked with the ropes. It began to squeeze itself through the hole in the egg. With a loud and sudden CRACK, the shell shattered and fell in pieces around its feet.

"It's out!" Eddy yelled. "Are you ready?"

"Nearly," Hen replied. "Just one more knot."

The chick shook itself out, feeling its way into its newly hatched body. Its first downy fluff was still damp and plastered to its skin. And then it stood upright for the first time, already taller than a grown man.

It fixed Eddy with a stare that reminded him of a crocodile – cold, calculating and deadly. And it started to move towards him. With its wobbling waddle, it looked less like a bird and more like a giant wind-up walking dinosaur toy. But there was nothing playful about the sharp beak that it held open as it headed unsteadily in their direction.

"We've got to move," said Eddy. "Come on."

They dragged the wings over to the edge of the nest, and hoisted them onto the rim.

"Turn round and face me," said Hen, "so I can tie your wings on. And tell me if that bird's getting close."

She fumbled with the long tails that she had left on the ropes, wrapping them over Eddy's shoulders and across his chest, round and over again and knotting them tight so that the wings were secure.

"Done," she said.

"Now you," said Eddy. "And quickly."

The chick was getting closer, snapping at the air with its beak.

Hen turned.

"There isn't time to put my wings on," she said. "If we try, it's going to get both of us. You've got to go."

"No," said Eddy. "I can't leave you."

"It's better that one of us manages to get away," said Hen, her voice catching in her throat. "Go."

Eddy pulled himself up onto the rim of the nest.

"Come here," he said, dragging Hen up after him. "I'm not going anywhere without you." He held his arms out towards her. "Oh dear. Look. I know you're a girl and stuff, and I'm a boy and…" He could feel himself blushing. "And my hands are all covered in bird muck… But do you mind if I…um…hug you?"

"Yes, I do," said Hen. "I know what you are doing. And we don't even know if these wings will take the weight of one of us, never mind two. Just go."

The chick was almost on them, its beak jabbing towards Hen.

"Well, then, I'm very sorry," Eddy stammered.

He grabbed her with both arms.

"I said no," said Hen. "Save yourself."

But Eddy held on to her as tightly as he could.

And jumped.

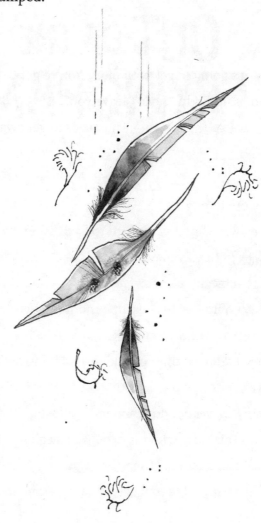

OUT OF THE FRYING PAN

They were falling.

They were holding on hard to each other, the wind was WHOOSHing in their ears, and they were falling fast through a bright, clear sky.

Eddy could feel his heart pounding in his chest. And Hen's heart pounding against it.

They had tried their best idea, and it looked like it just wasn't best enough.

Flap, flap, splat, Eddy thought.

Or in this case, whoosh, whoosh, bash.

And then suddenly there was a pull on his shoulders, a pull that tugged them back so hard that he thought his arms might be dragged from their sockets.

And then the wind was not whooshing so strongly.

And they were floating.

"They work!" Eddy yelled. "The wings work! Wooooooo-hooooo!"

"Ow!" said Hen. "That was right in my ear. But I'll let you off. Wooooooo-hooooo!"

"Any idea how to steer?" said Eddy.

"That's something for the mark 2 design," said Hen. "We just have to hope the wind treats us kindly."

It did.

They began to spiral downwards, towards the open plain.

"I've thought of something else for mark 2," said Eddy. "Landing gear. Hang on!"

The ground rushed up towards them. Eddy felt it scrape against his toes, and started running as fast as he could. The wind lifted them again for a moment, and then they crumpled down and slid across the dry floor. One wing snagged on a large rock, spinning them round as they came to a halt.

They let go of each other and lay on their backs, with the sun on their faces.

"I feel a bit sick," said Hen. "It was all that looping round that did it."

"Sick is good," said Eddy. "Because it means we're alive."

Hen sat up slowly.

"I'm afraid you've got a lot of bird poo on your back," said Eddy. "From where I was holding on to you with my grubby hands."

"Never mind that," said Hen. "We did it."

"You did it," said Eddy. "With your brilliant design."

"We did it," said Hen. "With your idea."

"Hey!" Six appeared from behind a nearby pile of boulders, followed by Claudius, with Mitzee on his back. "We saw you coming down. That was amazing. Are you okay?"

"Very okay," said Eddy. "But we need to get out of here and away from those birds. I don't want to have to go through anything like that ever again."

"Keep to where the boulders are," said Six. "We can pick a path through them. That way, the birds won't be able to see us most of the time. And if they do see you, you can huddle between the big stones where they can't reach you."

And that was how they made their way across the
plain towards Grimglower Castle. Three times they
saw a great bird circling overhead and hid from view,
and once they were spotted and had to take shelter
until their attacker gave up trying to grab them. But
eventually they left the plain behind, and travelled
along a green river valley until they arrived safely at
a clump of trees that gave them a clear view of the
castle.

It stood on a hill ahead of them, a sprawling, squat black building surrounded by a tall wall. A large iron gate set into a guard tower offered the only entrance.

"Now," said Eddy. "We need to work out how to get in."

"Piece of cake," said Six. "These people are amateurs. Over there." He pointed to a stretch of wall. "See that fig tree? You can put up as much wall as you like, but if you leave a tree growing just outside like that, you might as well post a big sign saying 'Come on in'. We climb the tree, hop over the wall, and bingo. All we need is a distraction to make sure the guards at the front gate are looking the other way."

"That sounds like a job for me," said Mitzee.

"Are you sure?" said Eddy. "What are you going to do?"

"You'll see," said Mitzee. "I can be very distracting when I try. "

"But first we'll have to sit here quietly and wait for it to get dark," said Six. He glanced up at the sky. "It shouldn't take long. Round here the sun sets very sudd—

—enly."

Eddy, Hen and Six watched from a distance as Mitzee led Claudius towards the front gate of the palace.

"Halt!" shouted a guard. "Sorry, miss. But you can't come in without a pass."

"I don't want to get in," said Mitzee, with a sob. "I just need some help. I think my camel has got a puncture, and I've no idea what to do. Boo-hoo, boo-hoo."

"Why does she have to pretend to be like that?" said Hen. "*I'm a girl so I'm just pretty and helpless!* It's rubbish. She was just the same with that man at the shoe stall in the market."

Mitzee was already surrounded by guards who were all eager to sort out her problem – and paying no attention to anything else around them.

"Rubbish or not, it's working," said Six. "Time to go." Leaving Mitzee and Claudius to their job, he ran towards the fig tree in a low crouch. Eddy and Hen followed. It took seconds for them to clamber into the branches, hop onto the top of the wall, hang down on the other side and drop to the ground.

"And there we are," said Six. "What did I tell you? I may be getting old, but I've still got it."

At that second, a glare of light flooded the patch of ground they were standing on.

"Actually," a deep, gruff voice boomed, "I think you'll find that *we've* got *you*."

AND RIGHT
INTO THE FIRE

Eddy peered through the glare of the light that was shining in his eyes. He could just make out the figure of the big, burly guard who had spoken. He could also make out the shape of the long sword in his right hand. And the other guards standing behind him.

"The old fig tree trap," the Chief Guard said. "Works every time. We don't even bother posting anyone around the rest of the palace. Everyone who tries to break in comes that way thinking they are being really clever. Until we grab them."

"Ah," said Six. "Ooops."

"But we weren't breaking in," said Eddy, trying to think of something that might get them out of the mess they had just blundered into. "No…um…our kitten climbed up the tree and fell over the wall and we came to look for her. Have you seen her, please? Small? Tabby? Mews a lot?"

"Yeah, right," said the Chief Guard, utterly unimpressed. "Still, it makes a change. Most people say they've kicked their ball over. Come on, we're taking you to see the Duke."

Surrounded by guards and with no chance to escape, Eddy, Hen and Six tramped down the dark passageways of Grimglower Castle. From floor to ceiling everything was black. About as black as the thoughts in Eddy's head.

He remembered how sour the Duke of Grimglower had been when they had met him in the Emperor's palace. Then again, he thought with a sudden burst of hope, the way the Emperor had treated him was enough to put anyone in a huff. Maybe the Duke wouldn't turn out to be so awful after all.

"How is the Duke today?" he asked. "Is he in a good mood?"

"HA!" the Chief Guard snorted with laughter. "Good mood? The Duke? Hey, lads, how can you tell if the Duke's grumpy?"

"Check if he's breathing!" the guards chorused back.

"I heard he's in a particularly bad mood today," said the Chief Guard. "Something to do with a tin of baked beans he can't open."

"Why doesn't he just have spaghetti hoops instead?" asked one of the guards.

"If your brain was any smaller," the Chief Guard said to him, "we could stick you in a pot and use you as a plant. Hup, two, three, four!" he added, in time to their marching.

"You're in trouble, that's for sure!" the guards responded.

"Five, six, seven, eight!"

"You're going to meet a dreadful fate!"

"That's really not helping," said Eddy.

"I know," said the Chief Guard. "That's why we do it."

They rounded a corner and entered a huge room. The Duke was sitting on a raised platform. His right foot, which was wrapped in a black bandage, was resting outstretched on a small black stool. Attendants clustered round him.

"Halt!" the Chief Guard instructed his men. "Your High and Mighty Worshipfulness, may I—"

"Can't you see I'm busy?" the Duke shouted back, without so much as a glance in his direction. "I've got a tin that I can't open and my foot hurts!"

"He tried kicking the tin earlier," one of the attendants muttered to the Chief Guard. "It didn't go well."

"So," said the Duke, "we have tried hammering this tin, we have tried drilling into it, we have attacked it with saws, dropped rocks on it from the tallest tower in the castle, had guards jump up and down on it in heavy boots, shot it with muskets, beaten it with sticks, poked it with pickaxes and had an elephant sit on it – how is the elephant, by the way?"

"Bottom still very sore, Your Mightiness," one of the attendants replied, "but the ointment seems to be working."

"HMMPF!" the Duke hmmpfed. "Have I missed anything out?"

"Kicking it, Mightiness," said another attendant.

"Which we will not mention again," said the Duke. "And after doing all that there is still not a single scratch, not a single dent, and not a single crack in this wretched tin. Has anyone got any other ideas?"

"Yes, Mightiness," came a voice from the ranks of the guards. "Spaghetti hoops."

"Take whoever that was," said the Duke, "put him somewhere dark and damp and feed him bread and water for a week. Oh, and make sure that wherever you put him has got lots of spiders in it. Now – anyone else?"

"I think I have the answer, Mightiness." A man wearing a shining breastplate and helmet stepped forward. There was a drumming of footsteps and rumble of wheels on the black marble floor, as a group of soldiers appeared through a doorway. They were hauling a carriage with a long cannon mounted on it, its mouth shaped like a dragon's head.

"I present the pride of the army, the mighty thunderer, frightener of foes and spitter of fire – the dragon cannon! I propose that we load the tin into it and fire it at the wall. Surely nothing could withstand such a blast?"

"Then what are you waiting for, General?" said the Duke. "Get on with it."

On the word of command, the soldiers pointed the cannon at the far wall of the room. Then they pushed the tin into the cannon's open mouth, rammed it down the barrel, lit the fuse and stood back.

There was a flash of flame, an almighty

BOOM,

a thunderous
CRACK,

and a billow of smoke. The boom echoed off the marble walls, setting Eddy's ears ringing, and almost deafening him.

Almost.

He could just hear the Duke shouting.

"That noise has given me a terrible headache! My foot hurts and I've got a terrible headache!"

The smoke slowly cleared, revealing the far wall. With a bit missing.

"You've blown a hole in my castle!" the Duke yelled. "My foot hurts, I've got a terrible headache and there's a hole in my castle! I hope for your sake, General, that you've done the trick with that tin. Go and find it!"

The gun crew clambered through the hole in the wall, bumping into each other and getting wedged together as they tried to get away from the angry Duke as quickly as possible.

"Now then!" the Duke spun round on his chair to see what was so important that the Chief Guard had interrupted him. His sore foot fell off the stool it had been resting on and bumped on the ground.

"Ow! I really, *really* wish I hadn't done that," he shouted. "So who have we got here then?" He looked down at Eddy, Hen and Six.

Eddy sensed that this might not be absolutely the very best time to be brought in front of him.

And he was right.

WELL – BUT WORSE

"They broke in," said the Chief Guard.

"I tried to explain," said Eddy. "Our kitten climbed over the wall…"

"Liar, liar, pants on fire," said the Duke. "Do I look like a fool?" He stared hard at Eddy. "I've seen you before. And the girl. You were at the Emperor's palace. I suppose he sent you to get his genie back. Are you really the best he could find? Two children and an old man?" He snorted down his nose, making a sound that was almost a joyless laugh. "Well, he's going to be very, very disappointed."

"We've found the tin!" a voice yelled from the far end of the room. The General trotted up, puffing slightly from his short run.

"Did it work?" said the Duke. "Is it open?"

"Um…" the General hesitated. "Not quite."

"How not quite? Battered? Dented? Scratched?"

"It's a bit sooty on one side."

"Sooty! That's *not* not quite! That's nothing! Give it to me."

The General handed it over. The Duke held it up.

"This is what you came for, isn't it?" He waved it in front of Eddy, Hen and Six. "Well, you're not going to have it."

"It's no use to you," said Eddy. "You'll never get the Genie out. Why not do the decent thing and give it back to the Emperor so he can carry on providing everything his people need?"

"I'm not interested in decent," said the Duke. "Decent is weak – just like the Emperor and his pampered people. Treat them mean, that's my way. If I can't have the Genie, nobody will. You see that hole over there?" He pointed across the room to where a large iron grate had been placed over a dark, round opening in the ground.

"The old castle well. Do you have any idea how deep it is?"

"No," said Eddy. "But…"

"Quiet!" shouted the Duke. "General! Take this wretched baked bean tin and drop it down the well."

"Wait!" said Eddy.

But the General didn't. He took the tin, trotted over to the well, pulled back the grate, and dropped it.

There was silence for a few seconds.

And for a lot more seconds.

And it still
hadn't
quite
finished.

And then
a
distant
SPLASH!

"That's how deep it is," said the Duke. "Deep enough to make sure that tin and its genie will never be seen again."

"Why…?" Eddy began.

"Stop bleating," said the Duke. "Guards, take them away."

The guards grabbed Eddy, Hen and Six by the shoulders and marched them out of the room.

They were just passing through the doorway when the Duke called after them.

"Oh, and I almost forgot. Execute them at dawn."

"I'm sorry," said Eddy. "It's all my fault. First the mess in Tidemark Bay, and now this."

He, Hen and Six were sitting on the floor of a dim and dusty room in a far corner of Grimglower Castle. Two guards stood inside the room by the door.

No one replied to Eddy. Hen and Six were too scared and gloomy, and neither of the guards had anything to say. The only sound in the room was one of a stone rubbing along the blade of a sword as one of the guards sharpened it.

"Could you stop that, please?" said Eddy. "It's really

getting on my nerves." He was trying to think of something – anything – that might get them out alive. But all that was in his head was that repetitive rasping sound.

"Bit touchy, aren't you?" said the guard.

"Are you surprised?" said Eddy.

"And after all we've done to make you comfortable," said the other guard.

"Comfortable?" said Eddy.

"You've got your bed, haven't you?"

"It's a blanket on the ground," said Eddy.

"That's all we get," said the guard. "If it's good enough for us, it's good enough for you."

"Besides," said the second guard, "it's only for one night."

The pair of them chuckled.

"What about a last wish?" said Six. "Don't condemned prisoners always get a last wish?"

"Go on, then," said the first guard. "Tell us what it is and we'll see what we can do."

"You're going soft," said the second guard.

"I'll tell you what I want," said Six. "I want to swap places with you." He pointed at the second guard.

"Nice try," said the second guard. "No chance."

"What about you two?" The first guard looked at Eddy and Hen. "Have you got any last wishes?"

Wishes, thought Eddy. It was wishes that had got them into all this in the first place. What could he do with a wish now? No magic this time. But could he trick the guards into bringing something that they could use to get out of there? This was his one chance. He racked his brain trying to come up with an idea.

And then he had a thought. Something that might just work. Something that the guards would never suspect was an escape plan.

The trouble was, it would take two wishes. And he only had one. The only way it was going to work was if he could get Hen to understand what he was trying to do, so that she would use her wish in the right way.

But how? He couldn't just whisper in her ear. The guards would instantly know that something was going on. He would have to give her a clue. A hidden clue that she would understand but that would mean nothing to the guards.

He turned the problem over in his brain. He poked it, and prodded it and walked round it to have a look at it from the other side.

After half an hour, when he decided he had done all the thinking that he could, and that this was the best idea he was going to get, he said, "I've got a last wish."

"You took your time," said the first guard. "Go on."

"Somewhere near the entrance to the castle, there's a girl with a camel."

"Don't tell me," said the guard. "You want to say goodbye to her? That's sweet."

"No," said Eddy. "I want to say goodbye to the camel."

"Really?" said Six. "That's the thing you want most?"

"Definitely," said Eddy.

"If it means that much to you I suppose we can try to find your camel," said the first guard.

"Bit odd, though," said the second guard.

"You understand why, don't you, Hen?" said Eddy. "I mean, he led us a bit of a *dance* at first, but we just *clicked* and had a really *smashing* trip."

He said it as clearly as he dared, and hoped that she really did understand.

Hen said nothing.

Come on, thought Eddy. *Please.*

He felt like he waited for ages. But…

"I've got a wish, too," said Hen. "I'd like to play the castanets one last time."

Yes, thought Eddy. *Well done, Hen.*

"Castanets?" said the first guard.

"My passion," said Hen. "I live to clack."

"There must be a pair in the room where the castle band keep their instruments," said the first guard. "So, last wishes. One camel. Some castanets. Weird."

"Yeah," said the second guard. "Kids these days, eh? I'll go and see what I can find. You wait here and watch them."

THE
LAST WISH

Claudius ducked his head as the guard led him through the doorway and into the room where Eddy, Hen and Six were being kept prisoner.

"Hello, old fellow," said Eddy, hugging his neck. "It's so good to see you."

"Are you feeling quite well?" said Claudius.

"He talks!" said the second guard. "That's cute."

But they didn't think he was cute for long.

Hen took the castanets from the first guard, and gave them a gentle CLICK.

Claudius's ears twitched.

Eddy quietly pulled Six into the far corner of the room.

Hen gave a louder CLACK.

The camel's front legs trembled.

She began to tap out a regular rhythm – three long clacks and two short –

CLACK-CLACK-CLACK-
CLICK-CLICK

A tremor ran through Claudius's body. His head shook. His neck rippled. His back wiggled and his bottom waggled.

"What's going on?" said the first guard.

Too late.

The beat was in control.

CLACK-CLACK-CLACK-
CLICK-CLICK

Claudius kicked out with a back leg.

One front foot shot out sideways.

He started twisting and turning, clattering across the floor, feet flailing in all directions.

CLACK-CLACK-CLACK-CLICK-CLICK

And suddenly there was an awful lot of camel and not very much room in the room.

"Duck!" shouted Eddy, diving out of the way.

"Hey!" shouted the first guard.

"Stop that!" shouted the second guard.

They tried to grab Claudius's harness and hold him still.

Big mistake.

CLACK-CLACK-CLACK-CLICK-CLICK

A flying camel foot caught the first guard on the chin, knocking him out cold.

CLACK-CLACK-CLACK-CLICK-CLICK

A swinging camel
bottom walloped the
second guard into
the wall, and he slid,
unconscious, to
the floor.

Hen stopped playing. Claudius came to a rest. He looked at the two flattened guards.

"Oh, dear," he said. "I hope they aren't damaged. One simply cannot resist that sound. Terribly sorry."

"Don't be," said Eddy. "You just saved our lives. Now let's get out of here."

A crescent moon shone in through the castle windows, giving enough light to see their way. They hurried down a long black passageway.

"We need to get our bearings," said Eddy. He reached into his pocket and pulled out the plan of the castle that the Emperor had given him. "The trouble is, these black corridors all look the same. We need something that stands out."

They turned the corner. And skidded to a halt.

In a room straight ahead of them stood a huge black statue of the Duke. The sculptor had captured him kicking an unfortunate servant up the backside. "I wonder if that's on the plan," said Eddy.

It was.

"So now we know we're here." Eddy pointed to the plan. "And the big room with the old well is marked over here." He pointed again. "It shouldn't take us long to get there."

"What do we do if we bump into any guards?" asked Six.

"Remember the Chief Guard said that they always catch people by the fig tree, and don't even bother posting men round the rest of the palace," said Eddy. "So with any luck we won't have a problem."

They found the old well. And, as Eddy suspected, they did it without being spotted.

But now they did have a problem.

Hen pulled back the grate and shone her torch down into the well. They could just see a faint glitter of water.

"There's no way anyone can clamber down there," Eddy said. "The walls are far too smooth. I was hoping there would be a bucket on a rope lying around that I could be lowered down on. But there's nothing – I suppose it's the old well and they don't use it any more. I don't know how we are going to reach that tin. Six, you're the proper thief. What do you think?"

"Whenever I was trying to steal something that was really hard to get to, I had a solution that always worked," said Six.

"Sounds promising," said Eddy. "What was it?"

"Give up and pinch something else instead," said Six.

"That's no good this time," said Eddy. "We could really do with a bit of magic now to get that tin back."

"Magic's okay," said Hen. "But sometimes what you need is a bit of science." She reached into her tool bag and pulled out her magnet. "Very useful for picking up stray screws, nuts, bolts – and baked bean tins. I just hope my ball of string is long enough."

She tied the magnet securely to the loose end of the string.

"Let's fish," she said, as she began to lower the magnet into the well. Eddy shone the torch down, and they watched the magnet drop and drop until it dipped into the water and disappeared from sight. A few seconds later Hen felt the string go slack.

"I've reached the bottom," she said. She jiggled the string, dragging the magnet around. "I felt a tug. I think I've caught something."

Slowly and carefully, she began to haul the string back up.

"There's something there," said Eddy. "But I can't tell what it is yet. Keep pulling, it's nearly…oh."

The thing came clearly into view. It was a battered trumpet.

"I wonder what that was doing
down there?" she said.

"Maybe somebody kept playing out
of tune," said Six.

Eddy pulled the trumpet off
the magnet.

"Let's try again," he said.

They did. Several
times. And they found a
soup spoon, the frame of
an umbrella, part of a
guard's helmet and most
of a roller skate. And
then, at last...

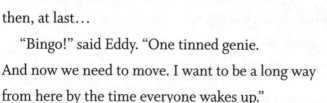

"Bingo!" said Eddy. "One tinned genie.
And now we need to move. I want to be a long way
from here by the time everyone wakes up."

They followed the plan of the castle, and were soon
at the front entrance. Mitzee was sitting on the ground
just inside the gate.

"At last," said Mitzee. "A man took Claudius away
and told me to wait here. I thought you were never
coming back."

205

"We nearly didn't," said Eddy. "What happened to those guards you were talking to?"

"They all went to bed," said Mitzee.

"That should make it easier to get out," said Eddy.

Unfortunately, before they went to bed, the guards had done something that was going to make it much harder to get out.

They had locked the front gate.

Everyone pushed as hard as they could, but they couldn't shift it by even a fraction.

"We'll never force it," said Eddy. "We need a key."

"Sounds like a job for me," said Six.

He slipped through a door next to the gate and into the guard tower. A few moments later, he slipped out again.

"Told you I'd still got it," he said.

The key he was carrying was as long as Eddy's forearm. Six slid it into the lock and turned. The bolt shot back. It sounded loud enough to wake the whole castle. But nothing stirred as they eased the gate open and slipped outside.

They closed the gate behind them, and Six locked it shut. Then he swung the key around his head and hurled it away into the night. They heard it clatter on a distant rock.

"Oops," said Six. "I seem to have dropped it. How clumsy of me. That should slow them down a bit if they try to come after us."

"Let's go," said Eddy. "And this time we're taking the quick road. If the Duke posted lookouts along it, they'll be watching for people heading *to* his castle, not away from it. We can be back at the Emperor's palace before word gets out that we've escaped."

A PILE
OF PANTS

Eddy was right. They reached the Emperor's city soon after sunrise. Lots of people were already up – and already grumbling. They had woken to find they faced another day with no fresh food. And no new clothes.

The men at the palace gate barely looked up as the group passed. They were too busy glumly taking turns to sniff at a small piece of cheese rind between munching mouthfuls of dry crackers.

Eddy led his party towards the doorway to the palace.

"I won't come in," said Claudius. "The Emperor still hasn't forgiven me for that time I wrecked his parade."

"Do you really think he's going to recognize you?" said Eddy.

"Most people can tell us camels apart, you know," said Claudius.

"Even so," said Eddy. "You saved us. That should more than make up for anything that happened in the past. Come on."

They found the Emperor in the golden room, chomping his way through a breakfast of sticky cakes.

"You're back!" he exclaimed, spraying a fountain of crumbs. "Have you got the Genie?"

Eddy held out the tin.

"I knew you could do it," said the Emperor. He tugged at the chain on his neck for the magic ring pull.

"You might have told us how difficult it was going to be," said Eddy. "And dangerous."

"I didn't want to put you off," said the Emperor. "Anyway, you're back now and that's all that really matters, isn't it?"

He pressed the ring pull against the baked bean tin.

"What really matters to me now," said Eddy, "is finding out from the Genie how we can get Tidemark Bay back to normal."

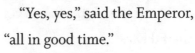

"Yes, yes," said the Emperor, "all in good time."

A puff of blue smoke emerged from the tin. As they watched, it grew into a cloud, which slowly solidified into the Genie.

"What is your wish, O master?" said the Genie. "And before you think of anything too complicated, can I just let you know that I'm feeling a bit dazed."

"Dazed?" said the Emperor. "You're a genie. It's not in your job description to be dazed."

"An elephant sat on me," said the Genie. "And they fired me out of a cannon. *That* really shook me up."

"It hasn't exactly been fun here either," said the Emperor. "I'm down to my last four days' supply of honey cakes. I was so worried about what I would eat if I ran out, I've almost wasted away." He stuffed another cake into his mouth.

If anything, Eddy thought, he was even rounder than the last time they had seen him.

"But I'll keep it simple," said the Emperor. "Just for you. And just for now. We must feed all the people in the city. Doughnuts. Everyone likes doughnuts. I want piles of them on every corner of every street. And the people will need something to drink. Orange juice. Let it rain orange juice."

"Really, master?" said the Genie. "That will make everyone very sticky."

"Then they will need new clothes, won't they? See to it."

"Yes, master."

"And the same for everyone in here," he turned to Eddy and friends. "You must be hungry." He noticed the state they were in and turned back to the Genie. "And you look like you need hot baths as well."

"And we need to know how to lift the curse on Tidemark Bay," said Eddy.

"Yes, yes," said the Emperor. "But baths first. There's rather a whiff of camel about you all and – ah, no wonder. Come out from behind that pillar."

Claudius stepped forward from his hiding place.

"Oh," said the Emperor. "It's you."

"You see," said Claudius. "I said he would recognize me."

"You are banned," said the Emperor. "I told you never to set your big clumsy feet inside this palace again."

"If it wasn't for him," said Eddy, "none of us would be here now. And you wouldn't have your genie back."

"Hmm," said the Emperor. "Then I suppose I'll have to let him off. But I really can't be doing with that pong. Genie – give him a bath, too. And send him back smelling of something more fragrant. Now off you all go to get washed and changed. I need to have a quiet word with my genie."

The quiet word that the Emperor wanted was about what should be done to punish the Duke of Grimglower. And they came up with an idea.

Back at his castle, the Duke had awoken that morning from a delightful dream about stealing sweets from small children. It had put him in the nearest thing to a good mood that he had felt for many months.

And then the day went downhill. First he learned his

prisoners had not been executed. And that a thorough search had been conducted in the palace and they were nowhere to be found. And that no search at all had been conducted outside the palace, because no one could open the front gate.

Now the Duke was in his worst mood for many months. Which was saying something.

He ordered the palace guards to line up in the main courtyard. He would find out who was responsible for these unacceptable events, and for making such a mess of his day. He stood in front of them, ready to let rip.

"This is a disgrace," he yelled.

And at that very same moment, the Genie put the Emperor's punishment into action.

"Who is responsible," the Duke bellowed, "for these unacceptable underpants?!"

The guards shuffled uncomfortably, looking puzzled.

"I'll ask you again," said the Duke, "who made such a mess of my underpants?!"

There were a few stifled giggles in the crowd.

"I don't mean underpants," said the Duke. "I mean underpants."

The giggles became louder.

"What's happening?" the Duke said. "Every time I try to say anything, it comes out as underpants."

A few minutes later, after he had ordered a hunt for the missing underpants, demanded an inquiry into how his underpants had escaped, and told the crowd that if they didn't stop laughing they would all spend a day with no underpants to eat, he realized that no one was paying any attention to him. They were all too busy rolling around on the floor helpless with laughter.

Ha-ha! Ha-ha! Ha-ha!
A-ha-ha-haaa!
Hee- hee! Hee- hee!

The Duke announced that he was tired, and had been working too hard recently, and was going for a lie-down in his underpants.

Which didn't help.

MAGIC RULES

"To raise the curse on Wizard Witterwort," said the Genie of the Baked Bean Tin, "the person who released him must make the Wizard's own wish come true."

"You mean me," said Eddy. "But you put the curse on him in the first place. Can't you just cast a spell, and sort it all out?"

Eddy, Hen, Mitzee, Six and Claudius had cleaned themselves up and gathered in the presence of the Emperor.

"There are ways in which these things must be done," the Genie told them. "Rules. Conditions. For so it is written in the Ancient Book of Magic. I can show you if you like." He pulled a massive leather-bound volume out of thin air.

"Blimey," said Six. "That was impressive."

"Let me see," said the Genie, thumbing through the pages. "Curses come between the chapter of spells to turn people into animals, and the one on getting difficult stains out of delicate fabrics."

"It's okay," said Eddy. "I believe you. Just tell me what happens next."

"First you must find out what the Wizard's wish is," said the Genie.

"I don't need to find out," said Eddy. "He's already told me. He wants his body back. Have you got a spell for that?"

"Of course," said the Genie. "But before I may cast it, the Ancient Book says that you must face a challenge."

"What sort of challenge?" said Eddy.

"I cannot say," said the Genie. "That is also one of…"

"…the conditions," said Eddy.

"Precisely."

"It's complicated stuff this magic, isn't it?" said Mitzee.

"Yes," said Hen. "Give me science any day."

"I shall ignore that foolish remark," said the Genie. "But only because you rescued me from the well."

"So this challenge you can't tell me about," said Eddy. "Does it just turn up? Do I get any warning?"

"You must present yourself at sunset on the beach at Tidemark Bay," said the Genie.

"Is that it?" said Eddy. "No hints? No tips?"

"Well, I shouldn't," said the Genie. "But as you also rescued me, I will say this. You possess three mighty objects of great power that will assist you. Do you remember what else was in the box when you bought the lamp and the statue?"

"Let me think," said Eddy. "There was an old toothbrush. That went straight in the bin."

"You must take it out of the bin as soon as you get home," said the Genie. "For that is no ordinary toothbrush. It is nothing less than the fabled Wand of Alacazar, a mighty weapon of great power that can smite your enemies with a fiery bolt of lightning."

"Really?" said Eddy. "Why does it look like a toothbrush?"

"What do you expect it to look like? It was easy in the old days. Everyone carried swords and daggers. You could dress up a magic weapon to look like one of those and no one would notice. But in these modern times you have to disguise them as ordinary everyday things. Like toothbrushes. What else was in the box?"

"A pair of wellington boots."

"The Boots of Instant Escape. When anyone wearing them is about to be struck a blow, the boots jump away before it can land. Anything more?"

"There was a cook's apron," said Eddy. "With roses on it."

"The ancient Robe of Unseeing," said the Genie. "The most magical of all the objects, for it renders the wearer invisible. These are three items of great mystery and power. Use them wisely and wield them well."

"If they are so brilliant," said Eddy, "what were they doing in a cardboard box at Tidemark Manor?"

"They were given many years ago to the owner of the Manor to hide and keep safe. It is a long and complicated story which there is no time to tell."

"It all sounds a bit crazy," said Hen. "But I suppose I should be getting used to that by now."

"Remember. The beach. At sunset," said the Genie. "And come alone. And now I will send you all back home."

"And you must take the camel with you," said the Emperor.

"That's very kind," said Eddy, "but to be honest, I haven't really got room for a camel."

"You misunderstand me," said the Emperor. "What I mean is, you *must* take the camel, or the deal is off. I'm not having him hanging around here any more, waving his feet about and breaking things. So, off you all go. Goodbye, everybody. And especially you," he said, taking Mitzee's hand. "We'll meet again – in my dreams."

"Bye, babes," she said. "That's sweet."

"I'll drop you all on the lawn," said the Genie. "You would never be able to get the camel down the chimney and out of the secret room."

"Hang on a minute," said Six. "I'm not with this lot."

He was too late. His voice echoed like a trumpet down a drainpipe. The room around them began to look blurred and smeary, as if it was a painting that was having water poured onto it. The smears began to form into new shapes – trees and bushes and grass – and suddenly they were standing just outside the front door of Tidemark Manor.

"I suppose," said Six, "that this means I'm going to be late home for tea."

READY
OR NOT

"We had better tell my brother we're back," said Hen. "He'll be wondering where we've been all this time."

They left Claudius munching his way across the front lawn, and went to find Chris P. He was waiting by the fireplace, exactly where they had left him. He sounded confused when they walked through the door.

"How?" he said. "Up the chimney...but not back... other way, then. So...passage just to outside? No secret room?"

"Yes, secret room," said Hen. "I'm not even going to try to rearrange the rest of what you said into a proper sentence. Where do you think we've been for the past two days?"

221

"Two days?" said Chris P. "Two minutes, more like."

"But we've been away," said Hen. "For ages."

"Not from where I'm sitting," said Chris P. "You've hardly been gone long at all."

"Really," said Eddy. "Where do you think our friend Six came from then?"

Six gave Chris P a little wave.

"Or the camel on the lawn out there," said Hen, pointing through the window.

"Or these fab clothes, Babes?" said Mitzee, twirling in her new outfit.

"When you say really," said Chris P, "you mean really *really*?"

"*Really* really." Eddy nodded.

"Well you might have told me," Chris P said, "so I could come with you."

"There wasn't a chance," said Hen. "We crawled down to the bottom of the bed in the secret room, and then we just fell into this foreign country. There was no way to come back to tell you anything."

"Bottom of the bed," said Chris P. "Right. I'm going to take a look."

"It's not the best time," said Eddy, "we've got loads of..."

"So you can do it, but not me?" Chris P interrupted. "I'm not having that. Hen, give me your torch so I can see where I'm going. And you two –" he gestured to Eddy and Six – "can give me a leg-up."

Eddy watched Chris P's feet disappear into the passage above the fireplace. A few seconds later they heard the squeal of the hinges on the trapdoor that opened into the secret room.

There was a brief silence. And then a loud BUMP as Chris P tumbled out of the bottom of the bed and landed head first on the floor.

"Ow!" he shouted. "I suppose you think that's funny, do you? Well, I knew it was a joke straight away – I only went along with it to show how stupid you all are!"

"I wonder why it didn't work for him?" said Hen.

"Maybe it only works when the Genie wants it to," said Eddy. "Anyway, I can't think about that now, I need to go to get ready for the challenge."

"I want to come with you," said Hen.

"I'd like that. But the Genie said I had to go alone," said Eddy. "Besides, you had better look after Six. He'll need somewhere to sleep. And Claudius. Don't let him near any stray castanets."

"Good luck," said Hen.

"I'll see you afterwards," said Eddy. "Tell you what happened."

If I can, he thought. *Because if the challenge – whatever it turns out to be – goes wrong, I might not see you ever again.*

Eddy opened the doors of the wardrobe in his bedroom. He stuck his head in, close to the vase that was sheltering Wizard Witterwort.

"I'm doing my best to get your body back," he said. "If everything goes well, it should happen quite soon. And if it doesn't happen quite soon, that probably means things haven't gone well."

He fished the Wand of Alacazar out of his wastepaper basket, brushed some fluff from its bristles, and stuck it into his backpack. Then he pulled the Boots of Instant Escape and the Robe of Unseeing out of their cardboard box, and packed them as well.

He glanced up at the statue of the Genie on his bookshelf. It cast a long shadow across the wall. The sun was already low in the sky. Nearly time to go.

He looked in on his mother in the front room – or at

least, on the young woman who was going to grow up to be his mother. Just thinking about that felt too weird. She was still asleep – getting young must be just as tiring as getting old. *Probably best that way*, he thought. At least she couldn't be confused or upset by what was happening if she wasn't awake.

Then he changed the channel on the TV.

"There you are, Dad," he said to the sofa. "There's some football on. And here's a snack for you." He stuffed a couple more digestive biscuits down the back of the cushions. "Hope it's a good match."

Then he quietly closed the front door behind him, and headed down to the beach to meet whatever was coming for him.

MAGIC HOUR

Weird things were still happening in Tidemark Bay.

As he walked down towards the harbour, Eddy passed a house where a spaniel was playing the piano, and singing in a beautiful clear voice.

In the next street was a cottage that was made entirely out of sweets. Three small children were bouncing round the front room, licking at the walls, while their mother sat in a corner quietly sobbing.

Down near the sea, all the lamp posts were wearing party hats. And there was a cheesy smell in the air. The ice cream in the harbour had started to melt, and the milk in it was going off.

Beyond the harbour there was a small park. A long strip of grass, dotted with flower beds, looked down on a stretch of shingle beach. Eddy plonked his backpack on a park bench and unzipped it. He tugged off his trainers and stuck his feet into the Boots of Instant Escape. They were several sizes too big, and came up almost to his knees. His feet flapped about in them when he tried to walk. Next he found the Robe of Unseeing and slipped it on over his clothes. Finally, he picked up the Wand of Alacazar and held it out in front of him.

I wonder if this just knows when to shoot lightning bolts? he thought. *Or do I need to press something to make it work?*

He turned it over in his hand and examined it. There were no switches or buttons. Its toothbrush disguise was perfect. He would just have to trust it to do what it was supposed to. But he could at least hold it like the mighty weapon it was. He practised his pose – one foot forward, arm out, brandishing it defiantly. That felt right.

And maybe he should say something. Something to scare whoever or whatever was coming for him.

"By the power of the fabled Wand of Alacazar…" he began. He felt a bit foolish. And sounded a bit wet. He needed to practise. He took a deep breath and started again, in the deepest, boomiest voice he could manage, "By the power of the Wand of Alacazar, I command you to begone – or feel its wrath!"

Wrath. He liked that word. It sounded good. Like something out of a superhero comic.

"Here, mate!"

"Mate!"

He looked round. A group of rabbits were sitting watching him, while nibbling at the flowers in the park.

"What you got there then, mate?"

"The Wand of Alacazar. It's very powerful."

"Expecting someone, are you, mate?"

"Or something," said Eddy. "I don't really know."

"Right. Here, mate, got any carrots?"

"No, I – hang on." A sudden thought struck Eddy. "You can see me?"

"Yeah. It's these eye things we've got stuck in our heads, mate."

"But I'm wearing the Robe of Unseeing. It's supposed to make me invisible."

"What did he say?"

"He said he's supposed to be invisible."

"Does he look invisible?"

"I don't know. I've never seen an invisible before."

"Sorry, mate, if we'd known you was invisible, we wouldn't have stared at you, would we, lads?"

Maybe I haven't put the robe on right, thought Eddy. *Or did the Genie say it made you invisible to enemies – so maybe rabbits don't count?* He was thinking about this when one of the rabbits spoke again.

"Flip! What's going on over there?"

Eddy turned back towards the beach.

He had never seen a sky like the sky he could see now. It was covered with purple clouds that seethed and bubbled like a vast cauldron of angry porridge. And beneath it, something was coming out of the sea.

It looked at first like the top half of a huge rusty iron ball, but as it rose from the water a face appeared, and then a neck and shoulders, and still it kept growing taller and getting nearer. Steam billowed from its ears, and its joints creaked and clanged as it took great strides forward. And now the metal giant stood on the stony shore, looming over Eddy, as tall as a church steeple.

Eddy looked up.

And up.

And then up some more.

He held the Wand of Alacazar out in front of him, his arm trembling, and began to speak the words that he had been practising.

"By the power of the Wand...."

At least, he tried to. But his voice stuck nervously in his throat, so it came out in a weedy warble, "Budda... pudda...wunna..."

And then his voice gave up completely, as the giant began to bend forward, lowering its head until it was just above him. With a whir of gears and a scrape of metal, its jaws opened wide, showing two sharp-toothed edges like giant saw blades. There was a hiss of air and then it spoke a single word.

ON THE
BEACH

Eddy's hand was trembling and damp with sweat. The Wand of Alacazar slipped from his grip and clattered to the ground. He scrabbled on the shingle to grab it again.

And then Eddy heard a high-pitched giggle. And a familiar voice.

"Oh, we so, so got you!"

A ladder slid down from the metal giant's open jaws, and the Emperor clambered onto the beach. The Genie of the Baked Bean Tin floated gently down behind him.

"Admit it," said the Emperor, "you were completely fooled, weren't you?"

Eddy admitted nothing. He just stood with his mouth hanging open, unable to find a single word.

"Loved the sky, by the way." The Emperor turned to the Genie.

"Thank you, master," said the Genie. "It's a little special effect I've been working on for a while."

"Does it come in any other colours?"

"There's this," said the Genie. He waved his hand and the boiling purple sky changed to a sickly yellow. "But I prefer the purple."

"Me, too," said the Emperor. "Anyway, put it away for now. And get rid of this rusty hulk. We're done with both of them."

The Genie clapped his hands. The sky cleared, and the giant metal figure vanished.

"This is just an ordinary old toothbrush, isn't it?" Eddy found his voice. "You've got me standing here wearing an ordinary old apron and ordinary old wellingtons and feeling like a total idiot."

"How you feel is your own business," said the Emperor. "But you are right about the rest. Getting you to think all this old rubbish was magic and dress up in it must be one of the best jokes we've played in ages."

"Well if this whole challenge thing is a joke," said Eddy, "would you mind just telling the Genie to give

the Wizard his body back and get on with
putting things back to normal round here?"

"No need to sound cross," said the Emperor. "And
the challenge isn't a joke. No, to lift the curse and all
that, you really do have to get through a challenge.
You've got to beat the Genie."

"That's what it says in the Ancient Book of Magic,"
said the Genie.

"Beat the Genie?" said Eddy. "At what?"

Does it matter what? he thought. *How can you beat
a Genie at anything?*

"Whatever I decide," said the Emperor. "Now, let
me think."

"I hope he doesn't ask us to build him a palace,"
the Genie whispered to Eddy. "He's always asking for
another palace. It gets so difficult to come up with new
ideas. I've done palaces of marble. Palaces of glass. One
made entirely out of clouds – that was rather good. And
one made out of cheese – that wasn't."

"I want you," said the Emperor, "to build me a
palace."

"Splendid idea, master," said the Genie.

"A palace of fun," the Emperor continued.

"A palace of entertainment. A palace to amuse me. We need somewhere for you to build. What if we just knock down this little town and start from there."

"But people live here," said Eddy. "And we want to put the town right, not make it worse. How about up at the Manor? There's loads of space in the garden."

"The Manor it is then," said the Emperor. "You've got twenty-four hours."

"What?" said Eddy. "We'll never do it in that time."

"It's always twenty-four hours," said the Emperor. "That's the tradition. I'm sure a bright lad like you will manage something."

"You've got magic on your side," Eddy said quietly to the Genie. "And I know how brilliant you are at that. We've got nothing to match it. But we did rescue you when you were stolen. So what I'm thinking is, maybe, could you do us a favour in return and let us win? Just so we can get the town back to normal? Please?"

"Let you win?" The Genie suddenly looked stern.

"The Genie Code requires every genie to always serve his master to the best of his abilities. No matter what he commands or why. I'm insulted that you even thought of asking me the question. So, no, I can't let you win. I shall be using all my magic powers."

"Then we've got no chance," said Eddy.

"No," said the Genie. "I don't suppose you have."

SOME HELPFUL ADVICE

"The only way we could build a whole palace in a day is by magic," said Eddy. He was sitting at home on his bed, talking to Wizard Witterwort's flimsy shape. "Is there anything you can do?"

"I'm afraid not," said Wizard Witterwort. "I told you. All I can do is answer wishes. One each for everyone in Tidemark Bay."

"And I suppose they have all used them," said Eddy.

"Actually, there is one left," said the Wizard. "But I don't know who it belongs to. I'll only know when I hear it."

"Maybe we could find out," said Eddy. "We could get them to wish for a palace…"

"It would probably come out wrong. My magic usually does."

"It would still be a start," said Eddy. "Something to work with."

The doorbell rang. Eddy went downstairs to answer it. He had phoned Hen and asked her to bring everyone from the Manor to see if they could come up with a plan.

Chris P pushed in past the others.

"I love little places like this," he said. "Just like proper houses – only smaller. Are we in here, then?" He strode through the door into the living room.

"No," said Eddy. "And don't sit on that sofa. It's my dad."

Chris P gave Eddy a hard stare.

"Yeah, right. I suppose he was an armchair when he was a boy and then grew up to be a three-seater?"

"Don't be stupid," said Eddy. "Come on. My bedroom."

"Your boyfriend's cracking up," Chris whispered to Hen as they climbed the stairs.

"He's not my boyfriend," said Hen. "And he's not cracking up. But even if he was he'd still make more sense than you."

"We might be able to get some magic to work for us," said Eddy, when Hen, Chris, Six and Mitzee had settled round his room. "There's one person in Tidemark Bay who hasn't used their wish. We need to find out who."

"Easy," said Chris P. "It's me. I just couldn't think of anything to wish for. I'm rich. I live in a huge house. I've got loads of stuff. I'm clever. And good-looking. And popular…"

"And wrong," Hen muttered under her breath.

"…I mean, what else could I want?"

"Fantastic," said Eddy. "We need you to wish for a palace. But you will have to think very carefully about what it looks like. We should probably draw a picture, so that as little as possible can go wrong when the Wizard makes the wish come true."

"And why should I do that?" said Chris P.

"So we can win the challenge and get everything back to normal," said Eddy.

"I'd just be giving my wish away," said Chris P. "What do I get?"

"You get to help everyone," said Eddy. "And you just said that you can't think of anything you want."

"Except that I just have," said Chris P.

"Got it," said the Wizard.

The room rippled gently.

A huge bag
of potato crisps
appeared in
Chris P's lap.
"Crisps?" said
Hen. "I can't believe
that you used your
wish on crisps, when you
could have helped us all."

"Maybe you should have thought of
that before you left me behind and played a trick on me
and made me bang my head," said Chris
P. "Maybe you will think of it next time
before you call me stupid and think
I'll fall for ridiculous stories about
furniture. Anyway, they are not just any
crisps. I wished that I could invent the
world's most delicious potato based
snack. And here they are."

He crunched into one.

"Oh, yeah, they are gooooooood.
Far too good to give away."

He stood up. "Right. I'm off. Have fun trying to save the town." And he stomped out.

"Sorry," said the Wizard.

"It's not your fault," said Eddy. "You can't choose what people wish for. But we've got a big problem with the palace. We'll never build anything in just one day."

"I don't want to be unkind, Babes," said Mitzee. "But you sound like those Whispering Sands. Can't, can't, can't."

"I'm trying to think of can, can, can," said Eddy. "I'm just not getting very far."

"What about that book you got from the auction?" said Hen. "The one with all the stories about genies and things. Is there anything in there that could help us?"

"I had a look through it before you arrived," said Eddy. "Couldn't find anything. But help yourself."

He handed the book to her.

"I can't read any of this," said Hen, flicking through the pages. "Oh, look. Here's that drawing of the guy jumping out of the tree. The one that gave you the idea of building the wings to escape from the nest.

You never told me what the story was about."

"I still haven't read that bit," said Eddy, looking over her shoulder. "It says – oh."

"What?" said Hen.

"It doesn't matter," said Eddy.

"Tell me," said Hen.

"Okay. It says, 'The story of how a foolish inventor made wings from giant feathers and broke every bone in his body. Warning. Do not try this at home'."

"And it was because of that drawing that we did try it," said Hen.

"Yes," said Eddy. "But we got it right. Which just shows that you must be a much better engineer than that inventor."

"Nice of you to say so," said Hen. "Hang on – what's this piece of paper in the front of the book? It says, Skirts – 2. Blouses – 3…"

"I remember that," said Eddy. "It's no use. It's just a list of things that Madeleine Montagu took on her trip."

"It's not just a list," said Hen. "There's a poem at the end. Listen."

"If you face your final challenge
And all hope seems to be dead
Just remember the solution
Is already in your head."

"That's nonsense," said Eddy. "If I had an answer in my head, I'd have found it by now. Unless… What if it doesn't mean this head?" He tapped his forehead. "What if it means – that head?" He pointed at the statue on his bookshelf. "Maybe she found out a way to beat the Genie, and hid the secret in there."

He picked up the statue and shook it. From its hollow insides came a faint noise.

"There is something in there," said Eddy. He turned the statue upside down and examined its base.

"Look. There's a circle of clay here that's a bit lighter than the rest. I think it's plugging a hole."

Hen pulled a hammer and chisel out of her tool bag and handed them to Eddy. He gave the clay circle a sharp blow. It pinged and shattered into fragments. He turned the statue the right way up again and shook.

A thin roll of paper fell out. Hen smoothed it open.

"There's writing on it," she said. "It's very small. And very faded. But I think I can make it out." She peered at the tiny letters.

She peered at the tiny letters and read aloud:

> *"Cheat. It's your only chance.*
> *Otherwise you are totally stuffed."*

"That's not as helpful as I hoped it would be," said Eddy. "How do you cheat when it comes to building a palace?"

"Nobble the other side," said Hen.

"He's a genie. How do you nobble a genie?" said Eddy.

"Steal someone else's palace?" suggested Six.

"From where?" said Eddy.

"Don't build a palace," said Mitzee.

"You can't win a palace building contest without a palace," said Hen.

"Except maybe you can," said Eddy. "I think I've got an idea. But we're going to need a lot of help. We need to get the whole town together for a meeting."

THE **IDEA**

They piled out of Eddy's bedroom. They knocked on doors. They spoke to people in the street. Eddy rang everyone he knew in town. And they asked them all to spread the message that there would be a meeting down at the Community Centre and that this was the only chance for Tidemark Bay to get back to normal.

Two hours later, a huge crowd had gathered.

Eddy climbed up onto the stage at the far end of the centre. The sour smell of the rotten ice cream in the harbour hit the back of his nose as he took a deep breath and began to speak.

"We've all seen weird things happening around town in the last couple of days. I'm here to tell you why – and, more importantly, how we have a chance to put it all right again. And I'm sure that's what we want, isn't it – to get everything back the way it was before?"

"What if we like it how it is now?" A voice came from one side of the crowd.

"I wasn't talking to you rabbits," said Eddy.

"Oh, charming, mate. Anybody got a carrot?"

"Perhaps some of you feel like those rabbits," said Eddy. "Maybe your wishes came out quite well."

"I got a new bedroom carpet," shouted someone. "And the pattern won't look too bad once I get used to it."

"My washing up does itself," said another. "And some of it hasn't broken."

"But a lot of people are in a mess," Eddy continued. "So the fairest and best thing for everybody is to lift the curse that has made all this happen."

A mutter of agreement ran through the crowd. But then, "What do you mean, curse?" someone shouted. "I thought this was all part of some TV prank show."

"That's right," said another. "We'll all be watching ourselves on the screen and laughing about it in a few weeks."

"My dad's turned into a sofa," said Eddy. "How could a TV programme do that?"

"Special effects," said a voice. "They can do anything these days."

"Believe me," Eddy said, "I know it's not a TV show."

"Course it isn't," said someone else. "We've all been hypnotized. None of this is really happening."

"It's the government," a man shouted. "They've put something in the water."

"I heard it was laser beams from mobile phone satellites frying our brains," said a woman.

"You're all wrong," said a man in a purple anorak. "It's a tear in the fabric of reality, made by mega-gigantic, multidimensional, super-intelligent zombie space squids who are eating their way in from a parallel universe."

"It's none of those," Eddy yelled. "It's magic!"

"Magic?" said the man in the purple anorak. "Now you are being ridiculous."

People started tutting. Some drifted away from the edge of the crowd.

"It's true," Hen shouted, clambering up onto the stage beside Eddy. "A few days ago I wouldn't have believed it either. But I've seen it with my own eyes."

Some more people started to walk away.

"Look," said Eddy. "I'll show you. This is the Wizard who is behind it all." He pulled the vase out of his backpack. Wizard Witterwort wafted out of it, green and wispy.

"Like I said, special effects," the voice came back. "And that one's rubbish. All blurry."

"Is that the best you can do?" someone else shouted. "This is just a bunch of kids messing us around."

"They aren't listening," Eddy said to Hen.

People were leaving in groups. The crowd was getting thin.

But then a woman put her hand up.

"I believe you," she said. She put her other hand up. "Magic is the only possible explanation for things like this." And then she put her other hand up. And the other one, as well. Sophie Milldew was not walking away.

"Me too," said Jeremy Grubb, pushing his wheelbarrow full of hair.

There were about fifty of them in the end – many of them bearing the signs of wishes that had gone wrong. Fifty people who stayed to hear Eddy explain all about the curse, and how it would be lifted if they beat the Genie of the Baked Bean Tin in a contest to build a palace.

"No problem," said a man in the middle of the crowd. Eddy noticed that he had screwdrivers where his fingers should have been. "I can see you're looking at these," the man said, holding his hands up. "I wished I always had my tools in my hands instead of having to search for them in my tool bag. I'm a builder, see. I can put up a palace for you. How long have we got?"

"It has to be ready tomorrow," said Eddy.

"You're having a laugh, aren't you?" said the builder. "It will take weeks. Months."

"That's what we thought," said Eddy. "Which is why we have come up with a plan. We're not going to build a palace. We're just going to make the Emperor – he's judging the contest – believe that we have built a palace. It's called cheating. We're going to make two rooms look like a whole building. Hen will explain."

Hen unrolled a set of drawings.

"I've done these designs," she said. "We need to make some big wooden frames and stretch canvas

250

over them. They are our walls. We'll put doors in some of them, and use them to set up two rooms, with a door between them. We'll roll out carpet for the floors, and stretch cloth across the top for the ceilings. With me so far?"

They were.

"So here's how we fool the Emperor. He walks into the first room, looks around a bit, and then goes through the door into the second room. As soon as he's in the second room, we close the door behind him. We then take down the first room. We carry all the pieces round to the other end of the second room, and build them up again. When we open the door at the far end of the second room and he walks through, he will think he is in a third room. Why wouldn't he? He's moved forward, and there are four walls around him. But the third room is just the first room in a new place. And while he's in there, we take down the second room, move it to the other end of the third room, and suddenly we have room number four. And so on. It's like two people playing leapfrog – each room hops past the other one in turn. We can make room after room after room with just two sets of walls. We'll make them all look different by swapping round the carpets and ceiling cloths and decorations. The way I've designed it, it will all slot together really quickly."

"How quickly?" said Sophie Milldew. "Are you sure there will be time to do it while the Emperor's in each room?"

"It's a palace of fun," said Eddy. "We put some sort of entertainment in every room to keep him busy while we rebuild. We can give him a tour of a vast building that isn't even there."

"It's ingenious," said the builder. "Or maybe it's just plain daft. I suppose we will know which when we find out whether it works."

"So," said Eddy. "Are you all going to join us?"

They were.

"I can help with the walls. I'm president of the Tidemark Bay Amateur Dramatic Society," said Maurice Burbage. He had finally managed to get out of bed after his terrible shock. "We build things like that all the time for our stage sets. We have all the wood and canvas that you need."

"And you can have my curtains for the ceiling cloths," said the woman who lived across the road from Eddy.

"They're all enormous. Plenty big enough."

"I'd like to help with the entertainment." Everyone burst out laughing as a glum-looking young man stepped forward.

"I'm funny," Dylan Plimpsoll went on. Everyone hooted again. "Even when I'm not trying."

Eddy thought his sides were going to split.

"Sometimes I think it's especially when I'm not trying," Dylan said flatly.

Hen giggled so hard that she nearly fell off the front of the stage. Laughter rolled round the Community Centre.

"You," Eddy said, struggling to get his breath, "are definitely booked. Right, everybody. Go and get a good night's sleep. We'll meet early in the morning up at Tidemark Manor."

BUILDING
WORKS

Eddy was too anxious to get to sleep straight away that
night. But he was too tired to stay awake for long.

He dreamed about what was going to happen
tomorrow. About the Genie creating a magnificent
white marble building so beautiful that it made the Taj
Mahal look like a garden shed. And about the
Tidemark Bay team creating a jumble of wood and
canvas so rickety that it made a garden shed look like
the Taj Mahal.

Early in the morning he cycled up to the Manor.
The Genie was already at work when he arrived.
At least, he assumed that the Genie was at work.
Strange noises were coming from the middle of a great
ball of fog that hid whatever he was doing.

ABRACADABRA!
CRUNCH!
HA!
Alakazam!
KER-PLUNK
Hechizos!
BOING...
PTZZ...PTZZ...
WOOF!
EH...?

"Pay no attention to him," Eddy told his Tidemark Bay team. "Just concentrate on what we have to do."

And concentrate they did.

Hen led the construction team. Together they sawed and drilled and hammered and shouted rude words when they accidentally hit their thumbs.

Mitzee led the decoration team. Together they brushed and rolled and sloshed shades of pink and orange and purple and green across sheets of canvas and occasionally across each other when they got a bit carried away.

Eddy led the entertainment team. Together they sorted out who was going to perform when, and tried to stop laughing at Dylan Plimpsoll while they were supposed to be rehearsing.

"I wish I could help," said Wizard Witterwort. "I used to be able to make wonderful shadows with my hands. Rabbit, bird, elephant, all sorts. They were such fun. Of course, that was when I had hands. And a shadow."

"If we can pull this off," said Eddy, "you'll soon have them back."

By the middle of the afternoon, they were ready to

practise putting the rooms up and taking them down again. It was tricky at first. Walls wobbled. Ceiling cloths fell down on people standing beneath. They accidentally rolled out a carpet over a sleeping dog that had chosen the wrong place to lie down. By the time they got the hang of it all, there was only half an hour to go before the judging began.

Eddy ordered everyone back to their starting positions. They set up the two rooms, and stashed the spare furniture in a large tent to the side. Then they put up the fake front wall for the palace. The design team from the Tidemark Bay Amateur Dramatic Society had painted it. It was as good as anything they had ever made – which unfortunately meant that it wasn't much good at all. It might just have fooled a very short-sighted person who had forgotten their glasses. As long as it was dark at the time. But it was all they had.

The Genie stepped out of the giant ball of fog. He was followed by two men with big muscles. The muscles weren't the most noticeable thing about them, though. The most noticeable thing about them was the fact that they were grey from head to foot.

"They look just like the two statues from the bottom of the garden," said Hen.

"They **are** the two statues from the bottom of the garden," said the Genie. "I got them to help me with some of the heavy lifting. A bit of strength is always useful on this sort of job."

"And just what sort of job is it?" said Eddy. They still had no idea what was hidden inside the fog.

"You'll see," said the Genie. "Are you ready? The Emperor is on his way."

"How is he coming?" said Hen. "Driving?"

"You could say that," said the Genie. "He always likes me to lay on a spectacular entrance for him." He pointed up into the sky. "There he is."

Eddy and the rest of the Tidemark Bay team stood open-mouthed as they watched four winged white horses coming in low over the treetops, pulling a golden chariot behind them. To a fanfare of invisible trumpets, their hooves touched down on the lawn, and they came to a gentle halt.

The Emperor stepped down from the chariot.

"Nice wheels," he said to the Genie. "Very swanky."

"Thank you, O master," said the Genie. "And if you

think the chariot was swanky, wait
till you see the palace of fun that I
have made for you."

He twirled his hands in the air.

The ball of fog began to spin round and
round, faster and faster, forming a tall cone that
rose into the sky.

But no one was watching it go. They were all
staring at what had been hiding inside it.

A magnificent white marble building stood
on the lawn. It was so beautiful that it made
the Taj Mahal look like a garden shed. The two
walking statues twined their arms together and
lifted the Emperor as if he was in a chair.

"Do join us," the Genie said to the Tidemark
Bay team, as the statues carried the Emperor
towards the palace.

Eddy was feeling more worried than ever
as he followed. He knew that if the inside
of the Genie's palace was anywhere
near as good as the outside, the
Tidemark Bay team were in
trouble. *Big* **trouble.**

QUITE A **NICE** PALACE

The inside of the Genie's palace was not as good as the outside.

It was better.

Eddy's heart sank as the Genie showed them into an elegant hallway. A huge stained-glass window pictured the moment when the Emperor had surprised the Duke of Grimglower with a faceful of pie.

"Like it," said the Emperor, who was walking between the Genie and Mitzee.

They passed along an avenue of elegant pillars, and into a vast room that sat under a glass-domed roof. Brightly coloured birds flitted among the lush tropical plants that stood around its walls.

"Pretty," said the Emperor.

In the centre of the room, a beach of white sand led to a brilliant blue swimming pool the size of a small lake. A waterfall that cascaded down from a tall rock sent ripples across its surface.

"Cool," said the Emperor. "You can't beat a nice paddle when the weather's hot."

"And along here," said the Genie – by "here" he meant a passageway where rainbows of light glittered off the crystal walls – "are two fun ideas that were suggested by one of the local people."

The passage divided into two.

"On this side," the Genie opened a tall double door, "is what he called a state-of-the-art cinema system." Eddy peered inside. Rows of plush seats, maybe two hundred of them, faced an enormous screen.

"And on this side," the Genie opened a matching door, "we have the track for the go-karts."

"What are those?" said the Emperor.

"They are karts, master," said the Genie. "They go."

PT-PT-PT-PT-PT-PT-PT-PT...

The air was filled with the stutter of an engine, as a kart whipped round the corner of the track in front of them. It whizzed past, leaving only a whiff of hot oil in the air, and the echo of the driver's cry of "This is brilliant!"

The Genie paused for a moment until the air settled again, then said, "It is considered to be quite exciting, master."

"That looked like Chris P driving the kart," said Hen. "I'm sure of it. So not only is he not part of our team, he's giving help to the other side. What a rat! If I get hold of him I'll…"

PT-PT-PT-PT-PT-PT-PT-PT…

Nobody heard what Hen was planning to do to her brother, as he whizzed past on his kart again with a cry of "WA-HOOOOOOOOOOOOO!"

"So, is that the lot?" said the Emperor.

"Indeed, master."

"Well, not bad. Quite good. Nice waterfall. Love the stained glass. So," he turned to Eddy, "ready to show me your palace?"

"Could you give us a couple of minutes to get in place?" said Eddy.

"Happy to," said the Emperor. "It's a pleasure to

spend more time in such delightful company."

"You flatter me, master," said the Genie.

"I wasn't talking to you," said the Emperor. "And you know it, you old tease."

He took Mitzee's arm in his.

"That palace was magnificent," Dylan Plimpsoll said miserably. The rest of the Tidemark Bay team couldn't help laughing out loud, even though they were all feeling extremely gloomy about their chances of winning.

"This is hopeless," Jeremy Grubb said, fiddling nervously with his wheelbarrow full of hair. "How can we go on after that?"

"The show must go on," said Maurice Burbage. "That's what we say in the theatre. Teeth and smiles, everybody."

"He's right. This is no time to give up," said Eddy. "We're going to go out there and give it our best shot." He dipped his hand absent-mindedly into a huge bag of potato crisps that was standing open next to him, and popped one into his mouth.

"Hey, hands off," said Hen. "Those are for the snack fountain."

"Sorry," said Eddy. "Mmmm. Those are really good.

What's the flavour? It tastes a bit like beef and mint and cheese and ketchup and sausage and pineapple – it really shouldn't all work together. But it does."

"They're Chris P's," said Hen. "The ones that the Wizard made when he wished."

"You pinched them?" said Eddy.

"I pinched them," said Six. "He'd carelessly left them lying round in a padlocked box underneath the floorboards in his bedroom. Piece of cake to get them out. Nice to do a proper bit of thieving again – makes this whole trip worthwhile."

"Chris P's not going to help us, so I thought we should help ourselves," said Hen. "We needed some crisps for the fountain, and my dad never leaves any around the house. Never give anything away if you want to get rich, he always says. I'd better go and load them. And then I think we're ready to go."

As ready as we'll ever be, Eddy thought. But he didn't say that. What he said was, "Right, everybody. We need bags of energy. Total concentration. Heaps of fun. And then we can still pull this off."

He made it sound so convincing that he almost believed it himself.

THINGS GO OKAY

It all started well enough.

Sharon Dibble's really nice shoes chatted away as she led the Emperor towards the Tidemark Bay Palace.

"It's an honour to have you here today."

"And you're looking so well."

Distracted by talkative footwear on one side, and Mitzee on the other, the Emperor barely glanced at the badly painted front wall as he walked into the first room.

Eddy and Hen remembered how much the Emperor enjoyed his food, so they had filled the room with the smell of hot pies. To make the smell, they had cleverly used nothing more than a table full of hot pies.

With four hands to do the work, Sophie Milldew had quickly turned out a huge batch of baking. The Emperor immediately tucked in, and made appreciative noises through a mouthful of steak and mushroom.

Then Dylan Plimpsoll entered.

"Welcome," he said.

The Emperor laughed so hard that a chunk of the pastry he was chewing shot out of his nose.

Dylan Plimpsoll had given up trying to make jokes. He realized that it really didn't matter what he said. Anything would get a laugh. He picked up the Tidemark Bay telephone directory and started to read aloud.

"Abercrombie, Arnold, 26 Seaview Terrace – 71346…"

The Emperor held it together through the 7134. But that 6 was a killer punchline. He lost it completely, and rolled around on the floor shrieking with laughter.

As Dylan continued, the Emperor was reduced to a giggling wreck. Each name and number seemed like the funniest thing he had ever heard in his life – until the next came along and was even funnier.

By the time Dylan got to "Banerjee, Anish, 9 Tiverton Crescent – 88357," he was clutching his sides and kicking his legs in the air and howling hysterically.

"I'm going…to burst…if he…doesn't…stop!" he panted.

Dylan closed the phone directory.

"If Your Majesty would care to follow me into the next room," said Eddy.

The Emperor was gasping too much to stand up, but he managed to roll over onto his hands and knees and crawl through the doorway into the second room. Mitzee followed him, and Eddy closed the door behind them.

As soon as the door shut, Hen's team began to take the first room apart. The Emperor had no idea that was happening, as he clambered onto a sofa with Mitzee beside him.

"Please. No more jokes," he said.

"Not in here," said Eddy. "This will give you a chance to get your breath back."

Across the room stood a thin, sharp-eyed woman wearing a blouse and a long tartan skirt, surrounded by a dozen children in matching tartan smocks.

"Celia Chillworth," the woman introduced herself. Celia could be found every Saturday morning at the Community Centre running classes in Country Dancing at ten o'clock and Karate at eleven o'clock – and only occasionally getting the two mixed up.

"And now," she went on, "the Celia Chillworth Country Dancing Troupe present our Scottish Spectacular."

She pressed the play button on a portable music centre. A harp strummed, a guitar twanged, bagpipes skirled, and the troupe of tartan tinies began to twirl.

Eddy pressed his ear to the door. He could just hear Hen's team at work, getting ready to move the pieces of the first room to their new location and set them up as room three.

The Emperor was getting restless. Country dancing clearly wasn't his thing.

"I fancy more of those excellent pies," he said. "I'll just go back to the first room to grab a couple."

"NO!" Eddie yelled. "DON'T!" It would be a disaster if he went through the door and found there was no first room to go back to any more. Their whole plan would be blown wide open when it had barely started.

"Since **when** do you tell me what to do?" said the Emperor.

"I mean, please don't trouble yourself, Majesty," Eddy said. "I'll get them for you."

He opened the door a crack and squeezed through, careful not to give the Emperor a chance to see what was on the other side. Hen and her team were carrying the walls away.

"How much time is it going to take?" Eddy asked. "I don't know how long I can keep him in there. He's getting a bit bored."

"It's country dancing," said Hen. "Of course he's bored. But we need a few more minutes."

"I'll do my best," said Eddy. He picked up the pies, and squeezed back through the door.

"Very good," said the Emperor, grabbing his snack and starting to haul himself out of his chair. "I'll have these on the way to the next room."

"It's extremely bad for the digestion, Majesty," said Eddy. "Walking and swallowing at the same time. Much better to sit here and eat. Besides, you wouldn't want to miss the big finish to the routine." He doubted that a big finish was coming, but at least he had got the Emperor to stay where he was.

The Emperor gulped the
first pie down in two bites.
The twelve twirling tartan tinies
held hands and formed a ring, and
began to skip round in a circle –
until one of them snagged a
twirly toe in a crease in the
carpet. Down the tiny
tumbled, dragging its tiny
neighbours down with it,
and so on round the ring.
One after the other, twelve tiny
tartan bottoms hit the floor,
and twenty-four tiny legs in
tartan socks thrashed in the air.
"You were right," said the
Emperor. "That ending was
the best bit by far."

He swallowed the last of his second pie and headed for the third room. Eddy stepped ahead of him to open the door, hoping that Hen and her team had managed to finish putting the room together.

He breathed a sigh of relief. Everything was in place. And with a different carpet and some new decorations, it looked quite unlike the first room.

The new room housed a strange contraption. It had a broad metal belly studded with pipes and valves, and a tall shining funnel rising from its top. It looked like someone had cobbled together an old-fashioned stove, a vacuum cleaner and a trombone. Which was not altogether surprising, because that was exactly what someone had done. And the someone was standing next to it in her best boiler suit.

"Your Majesty," said Hen. "May I present a world first – the potato snack fountain!"

She clicked a switch with her foot. The machine let out a long wheezing sigh that rose in pitch and volume until suddenly:

PFFFFT!

A slim slice of deep fried potato shot out of the top of the funnel and fluttered through the air.

PFFFFT! PFFFFT! PFFFFT! PFFFFT! PFFFFT!

The middle of the room was filled with a cloud of cascading crisps.

Chris P's crisps. They looked like a fall of autumn leaves in a stiff breeze, but no leaf ever tasted like these.

One flittered down right in front of the Emperor's face. With a snap of his head and a smack of his lips, he crunched and swallowed.

"Absolutely *delicious*," he said. "I'm not leaving here until I've eaten every last one."

Eddy had never seen the Emperor move so fast. Come to think of it, he had never seen the Emperor move much at all. But here he was, trundling around the room, snaffling up every crisp he could find and stuffing them into his mouth.

"Well done," Eddy said to Hen as she slipped away to check on the building of the next room. "He loves it. If we carry on like this, we might even manage to pull off a win."

But as if the world had just been teasing the Tidemark Bay team all along, at that very moment things started to go wrong.

Dreadfully wrong.

BUT NOT FOR LONG

The Emperor licked the very last crumb of the very last crisp from the corner of his mouth.

"Yum!" he said. "Very interesting flavour. I must get the recipe. What's next?"

Eddy led him and Mitzee into the fourth room. In the middle of the floor stood a low couch, a large wicker basket filled with theatrical props, and Maurice Burbage.

Maurice had agreed to entertain the Emperor with extracts from his epic one-man performance, Great Moments From Shakespeare. He had decided to start as Hamlet, with the most famous speech of all – "To be, or not to be."

As soon as the Emperor settled his bottom in an armchair, Maurice took a deep breath, raised his right hand, furrowed his brow, and began.

"OHHHHHHHHHHHHHHHHHHHHHHHHHH!"

Shakespeare had not written that at the start of the speech, but as far as Maurice was concerned, there was no dramatic moment that could not be improved by a good "OHHHHH!" And sometimes, two.

"OHHHHHHHHHHHHHHHHHHHHHHHHHHH!"

he said again. "To be or…"

Hen and her team had hung several mirrors around the room, to make it look different from the others. Maurice caught sight of the Emperor's reflection in one of them. And then in another. And then a reflection of a reflection that made it look as if a long line of Emperors were all staring at him.

"To be or…" he repeated.

And suddenly the memory of the other night flooded through him. He was there again, standing in front of the huge audience in the National Theatre, with no idea what he was supposed to say, or do. His legs wobbled.

A drop of sweat ran from his forehead, down the length of his nose, and dripped onto the floor.

"To be…or…" he stammered, "be…or," a look of horror on his face as he relived his nightmare.

"Does it go on like this for long?" said the Emperor.

"Be…or…be…be…"

"Because I've had enough already." The Emperor rose to leave.

"The next room won't be ready yet," Eddy whispered to Mitzee. "You've got to keep him here."

"Be…be…do…be…"

"Me?" said Mitzee. "How?"

"Think of something," said Eddy. "I've got to tell Hen they have to hurry up."

"Be…do…be…do…" Maurice burbled.

"Hang on, Babes," Mitzee said to the Emperor, in a moment of inspiration. "I love this song." And she began to hum "Do-be-do, do-be-dooby-doooo," in what was almost a tune.

Eddy rushed out into the fifth room. At least, he rushed into where the fifth room was going to be. It was still a wall and a half short, and had no carpet on the floor.

"Quick," said Eddy. "You've got to be ready to go in one minute."

"No chance," said Hen. "We might get the walls up, but the carpet's still round the other side. We can't get it rolled out in time."

"We need to do something," said Eddy.

"Use me," said Jeremy Grubb, lying down on the floor. "You can spread my hair out. There's more than enough to cover it. It's good to find a use for it at last."

"Great idea," said Eddy. "Let's get the walls up. Everyone else, start hairdressing."

They began to haul out long strands of hair and spread them to cover the ground.

"It's still no good," said Hen. "What about the ceiling? The cloth's over with the carpet. We've got nothing."

Eddy looked up at a cloudy sky.

"We can tell him it's a glass roof."

A few drops of rain fell on his face.

"He'll never fall for it," said Hen.

"I've got a better idea." It was Celia Chillworth. "I can keep the Emperor entertained while you sort this room out properly."

"Are you sure?" said Eddy.

"I did twenty-eight years in cabaret on the cruise ships before I settled in Tidemark Bay. Of course I'm sure." She grabbed her music player and headed into the fourth room.

Maurice Burbage was huddled under the low couch, making occasional mewing noises.

"Time to go," the Emperor said to Mitzee. "This is all much too modern for me."

But before he could move a muscle, Celia Chillworth pinned him to his chair.

"Welcome to this celebration," she said, thrusting her face into his, "of the joyous spirit of fiesta and the traditional dances of Spain. After which I shall break a house brick in two with one chop of my bare hand."

"Now **that** sounds more like it," said the Emperor.

With a blare of trumpets, her music centre burst into life, and Celia began to stamp her feet and twirl her long skirt as she danced.

"That should keep him busy for long enough," said Eddy, who was listening from the next room.

But then.

CLACK-CLACK

"Did you hear that? said Eddy. "It sounds like castanets."

CLACK-CLACK

The sound wasn't just *like* castanets. It **was** castanets. Castanets that chattered between Celia Chillworth's fingers.

The noise drifted out through the thin canvas walls of the palace, over the heads of Hen and her construction team, and across the lawns and flower beds of the garden at Tidemark Manor...

...straight into the ears of Claudius the camel, who at that moment was contentedly chewing his way through a particularly tasty stretch of shrubbery.

At the sound of the
first CLACK, his jaw
froze in mid-chomp.

At the sound of the
second CLACK, his head
jolted upright.

By the third CLACK, he broke into an itchy,
twitchy dance that drew
him towards the
source of the
irresistible
sound.

He trampled through a patch of tulips, skittered across the lawn and crashed into the room that Hen and her team were building.

"RRRRRRIPPPPPP!"

went one of the canvas panels as his head came straight through it.

"CRRRRRACCCKKK!"

went the wooden frame as the rest of his body followed.

"JUST... CAN'T... CONTROL MYSELF!"

went Claudius as his legs flew out in every direction, scattering the building team.

"OWWWWWWWW!"

went Jeremy Grubb as Claudius's flailing feet got

tangled up in the long strands of his hair that had been spread out to carpet the room.

"AWFULLY SORRY!"

Claudius added as he continued on his unstoppable way towards the room where the Emperor was sitting.

"WHHHOMMMMPP!"

went the door into that room as Claudius slammed through it.

"EEEEEEKKK!"

went Celia Chillworth as she dropped her castanets and fled from the sweaty beast that was bearing down on her.

"CRREEAAAKKKK!"

went the wall that Claudius had just bashed as it began to tip forward.

"NOOOOOOOOO!"

went Hen, as she grabbed hold of the wall to try to stop it falling.

"LOOK OUT!"

went Mitzee as the wall carried on toppling towards them.

"PHEEWWWWW!"

panted Claudius as his body finally stopped twitching.

"BOMPPPPPPPP!"

went the wall as it hit the ground just in front of the Emperor.

"WELL, HELLO AGAIN,"

said the Emperor, as Hen landed face downwards, still clinging on to the fallen wall.

And

"SPLAT!"

went Eddy's hopes of winning the contest.

Everywhere Eddy looked, there was CHAOS. Claudius was tangled up in Jeremy Grubb's hair. Splinters of wood and shreds of canvas were strewn across the floor.

The whole thing was a MESS.

A DISASTER.

A FAILURE.

So terrible that the Emperor was rocking
with laughter.

"Well," said a voice in Eddy's ear. It was the Genie. "I don't think there's much doubt about which one of us has won. I'd like to say nice try. But it wasn't, really, was it?"

AND THE
WINNER IS...

Eddy felt sick. What had he been thinking? It had been stupid of him to imagine that they could ever beat the Genie. That canvas and paint could ever be a match for magic and marble.

So now the Wizard wasn't going to get his body back, and Tidemark Bay was going to carry on being crazy, and his mum and dad were stuck as a young girl and a sofa. He wondered if that made him an orphan? It certainly left him on his own.

"The winner of the contest is obvious," said the Emperor, when he finally stopped laughing at Tidemark Bay's terrible effort. "That white marble palace was beautiful. The stained glass gorgeous. The waterfall, the beach, the tropical gardens, all wonderful."

Okay, Eddy thought, *we know. No need to rub it in.*

"I asked for a palace of fun," the Emperor continued. "And fun is what I got. So the winner is... the **Tidemark Bay Palace.**"

"*What?*" said Eddy.

"*What?*" said the Genie.

"I've **never** laughed so much in my life," said the Emperor. "Oh, the marble and the glass and the pillars and the waterfall and the beach and the garden were all so tasteful. It took me a while to catch on to what the Tidemark Bay team were up to. But from the talking shoes and that tatty painted entrance to the awful actor and the big comedy finish, their rickety wreck was a hoot. Nice pies, too. And those crisps. Delicious."

"But..." said the Genie.

"No buts," said the Emperor. "**I'm** in charge. Give the Wizard his body back as we promised, and then we can all go home."

It took a matter of seconds for the Genie to cast a spell that restored Wizard Witterwort. His flat green shape solidified into a human figure. Who was still, rather surprisingly, green.

"Oh," said the Wizard. "You know, I was rather hoping that would have worn off after all these years. Another spell that went wrong."

"Get rid of the green," said the Emperor. "It's making me feel rather queasy."

The Genie cast another spell, and the Wizard's skin took on a natural colour.

"Thank you all for restoring me," he said.

"Can we put things straight round Tidemark Bay now?" said Eddy.

"It has already begun," said the Genie. "By tomorrow everything will be as it was."

"Splendid," said the Emperor. "All back to normal." He turned to Mitzee. "Well, my dear. It looks like this is goodbye."

"Don't tell me," said Mitzee. "All back to normal means I'm going to be a doll again. You're dumping me, aren't you? WAAAAAHHHH!" she began to wail.

"It looks like goodbye…" said the Emperor, struggling to make himself heard as Mitzee sobbed.

"WAAAAAAAAAAAAA…"

"…unless you will come back with me and be my Empress. Will you marry me?"

"WAAAAAAAAAAAA…of course I will, Babes." The wailing stopped as suddenly as it had started. "But I'm not going to be one of those palace wives who just sit around all day doing nothing. I've discovered my passion – interior design and decoration. And I can't wait to give your palace a good makeover. Those gold walls are so last year."

"But—" said the Emperor.

"No buts. We're going for something elegant and sophisticated – like me. I'm thinking Scarlet Splurge and Lime Zinger for the throne room. What do you say, Babes?"

"I—" said the Emperor.

"You'll love it," said Mitzee. "So that's sorted." She turned to Hen. "You don't mind, do you? Not having me here to talk to any more?"

"It's fine by me. Go and have a good life," said Hen. She looked at Eddy. "I've got a friend I can talk to now."

"Splendid," said the Emperor. "So, everyone has what they want. Except for one thing. Those crisps that were in the fountain. Delicious. I must have some more of them."

"I made those," said the Wizard.

"Really," said the Emperor. "Then do it again. You've got your magic back now."

"If your Genie will do something for me in return," said the Wizard. "Make this my last spell. Take away my magic. It just goes wrong and causes trouble. I don't want it any more."

"Make it happen," the Emperor said to the Genie. "Now – those crisps. I can't wait to taste that delicious beef and mint and cheese and ketchup and sausage and pineapple flavour again."

"Let me see," said the Wizard. "I think I can remember." He muttered a few words and clapped his hands together.

A ripple ran through the garden. A cow suddenly appeared on the lawn. It was chewing a large sprig of mint, and had a string of sausages hung round its neck, a potato stuck to one of its horns, and a stack of pineapple rings on the other.

"Ah," said the former Wizard Witterwort. "That didn't come out quite right."

"Hopeless," said the Emperor. "Genie, make me some crisps."

"Unfortunately, master, you ate every last scrap. I have nothing to taste so I can work out how to copy the curious flavour that you described. So I can't."

"But I want them," the Emperor shouted. "I can't have them and I WANT THEM!"

And then he stopped shouting. "How very interesting. How very tantalizing. Do you know what you people have done? You have given me the one thing in the world that the Genie could not. Something to desire. After all these years of being bored because I could have anything I could think of, there is now something I can think of that I can't have. I can't tell you how precious that feeling is."

It seemed that everything was coming good. But it wasn't quite over.

RIBBIT!

"What is going on in my garden?" a gruff voice called out. An angry-looking man in a pinstriped suit was stomping towards them.

"It's my dad," said Hen. "He must have come back from his meeting with the architect."

"Who *are* these people? What's all this mess? And what is that big white building?" Mr Crumb bellowed.

"And where are my crisps?" Chris P was trotting behind him.

"We can clear everything up in an instant," said the Emperor. "Genie, sweep up the mess and get rid of your palace."

"Wait!" said Eddy. "You're not just going to destroy it, are you? It's beautiful."

"Wait!" said Chris P. "You can't let him, Dad. It's got a cinema and go-karts and a pool and everything we want to add to this old place."

"Wait!" said Mr Crumb. "I heard what my lad said. It's on my land, and as far as I am concerned, that's means it's mine. Don't touch it. It will save us a fortune in builder's fees."

"It's not yours," said Hen. "You had nothing to do with it. It's only here because of all the rotten things that have happened to everyone in Tidemark Bay. If anyone deserves it, it's them. They should all be allowed to share it."

"Share!" shouted Mr Crumb indignantly. "SHARE! For nothing in return? I'll have you know, my girl…"

Hen never heard what he wanted her to know. And nor did anyone else. At a signal from the Emperor, the

Genie turned Mr Crumb into a frog. Everyone could tell it was him, because he was still wearing a pinstriped suit.

"RIBBIT!" said Mr Crumb.

"That's better," said the Emperor. "Much quieter. I think your idea of everyone sharing the palace is a splendid one. And your father obviously hates the thought of letting other people use it. Which makes it even more splendid. So, Mr Crumb, here is your choice. You can agree to let everyone share, or my genie will take it away, and then you will have to pay the enormous cost of building something new. One ribbit for no, two ribbits for yes. And then we'll turn you back into a human."

"He won't like that," said Hen.

And he didn't.

"I don't think I've ever seen an angry frog before," said Eddy.

Mr Crumb hopped round the garden until he went red in the face, turning over the agonizing choice between giving something away or spending heaps of money.

Finally he stopped hopping. He beat his front feet furiously up and down on the lawn for a moment. And then, "RIBBIT!" he said. "RIBBIT!"

"Excellent decision," said the Emperor, as Mr Crumb returned to his usual shape. "It's good to share. Of course, if you ever change your mind and want to stop other people using the palace…"

"Yes?" said Mr Crumb.

"…my Genie will change you into a frog again. So keep your word."

And that was how Tidemark Bay got its splendid new Leisure Centre.

"One last thing," said Eddy. "This building is only here because a long time ago the old owner of the Manor brought home Wizard Witterwort in his lamp. She was an incredible traveller, and I think she deserves to be remembered by the town."

"Genie," said the Emperor. "See to it."

And that was how the Tidemark Bay Leisure Centre got its splendid bronze statue of Madeleine Montagu on her pogo stick, hair and skirts flying, looking as if she was about to bounce right off her pedestal.

After that things returned to normal.

The Emperor, the Genie, Mitzee and Six went back to the Emperor's city. The Emperor even took Claudius with them. He had realized that he could have great fun with visitors by asking them to play the castanets when the camel was around.

Wizard Witterwort became plain Walter Witterwort, and stayed in Tidemark Bay. He missed living in his old lamp, but he soon found a home in a much bigger one, when he got a job as the curator of the Old Lighthouse Museum. On clear nights he sometimes fired up the antique light, and used it to make shadow puppets on the cliffs beside the bay.

Chris P never got his crisps back. But he spent all his spare time trying to recreate that mixed-up flavour that really should not have been delicious, but was.

As for Eddy – he went back home. When he woke the next day, everything in Tidemark Bay was back to how it had been before the wishes, just as the Genie had said it would be. He went downstairs. His parents were already sitting at the breakfast table, sharing a pot of tea.

"Everything okay?" said Eddy, pouring out a big bowl of his favourite Choccy Puffs.

"Fine," said his mum and dad.

It was as if nothing strange had ever happened. Almost.

"Except," said his dad, wriggling in his chair, "it's very odd. I keep finding digestive biscuit crumbs in my pants."

Eddy decided not to try to explain that one. It was a long story.

THE
END

ABOUT THE AUTHOR

Before he started writing children's books, Simon Cherry spent almost twenty years making television documentaries in the Arts Department at ITV. He has also written for newspapers, magazines and the stage. Simon lives in Surrey with his wife, two teenage sons, and a ginger cat who is in charge of everyone else. When not writing, he spends a lot of time looking at the garden and wishing it would weed itself. So far, this has not worked.

READ MORE EDDY STONE ADVENTURES!

To Susannah –
for all the magic.
SC

For Charlie, Millie and Freddie:
Sally's beloved great nephews and niece.
And for Tina's Freddie too!
FB

First published in the UK in 2018 by Usborne Publishing Ltd., Usborne House,
83-85 Saffron Hill, London EC1N 8RT, England. www.usborne.com

Text copyright © Simon Cherry, 2018
The right of Simon Cherry to be identified as the author of this work has been
asserted by him in accordance with the Copyright, Designs and Patents Act, 1988.

Illustrations copyright © Usborne Publishing Ltd., 2018
Illustrations by Francis Blake.

The name Usborne and the devices 🏆 🎈 are Trade Marks of Usborne Publishing Ltd.

A CIP catalogue record for this book is available from the British Library.

JFMA JJASOND /18

ISBN 9781474936750 04516/1
Printed in the UK.